DON'T GO DOWNSTAIRS

DON'T GO DOWNSTAIRS

A PSYCHOLOGICAL THRILLER

JACK DANE

CONTENTS

Enjoy your stay! There's only one rule...

After three decades of marriage, Deb and Larry are in a rut. So when the chance to spend a whole week at a **Long Island seaside cottage** comes up, they take it. A week on the beach could be just what they need. The best part? It's completely **free**.

There's just one rule: **Don't go downstairs into the basement.**

But soon after arriving at the beautiful home that belongs to a separated couple, a **hurricane brings rain and road-flooding** that **traps them inside** for longer than they'd like.

The longer Deb and Larry are forced to stay, the more they learn about the owners of the house. The loud arguments, the sudden separation. The fact **no one has seen the wife since**. As their questions grow, so does the temptation to break that one rule.

Because the only way to get answers is to go downstairs.

But if they do, the whole horrifying truth will be revealed.

PROLOGUE

Message from Kevin P. sent at 9:31 AM:

Super excited to initiate this house exchange. I think it'll be a really good thing for both of us. Just a few things I'd like to make you aware of before your stay.

The house...while beautiful, it definitely has its quirks. Part of the charm in living in an old farmhouse, after all. I've gotten used to them over the years, but for someone else, it might take a little getting used to.

For instance, there's a lot of odd sounds at night. And by odd, I mean sometimes downright spooky. You might start to think there's someone else in the home with you, but I assure you, it's just the house's old bones settling. Nothing to be concerned about, I promise.

Another thing— the doors might also be a little creaky. They might even open on their own. Another part of older house charms. Warped, old wood. Again, nothing to be too worried over.

While a little strange at first, I'm sure you, like I have, will learn to really love this place during the time you're here. In fact, I can practically guarantee it.

Feel free to use any and all silverware, plates, and glasses. Towels and fresh sheets are in the upstairs closet. I think I've got a few bottles of wine tucked away as well, if that's of any interest.

In terms of outdoor activities, I've got beach chairs, kayaks, and a beach umbrella on the porch. Please utilize those at your leisure. Basically, what's mine is yours. The bedrooms, the TV, the Adirondack chairs—feel free to use whatever you like.

Really, there's only one rule—don't go downstairs into the basement.

ONE

The distant siren brings my head up and my gaze to the window.

"Sounds like there's a fire nearby," I say over my shoulder as I draw apart the curtains.

Larry grunts but doesn't look up from his paper. Nothing will disturb the morning routine he's maintained for decades, apparently.

The newspaper crumples slightly in his grip as he turns the page, head out of view.

I let out a sigh and look down at my breakfast. I've been getting a lot of grunts from Larry lately. Or maybe it's been like this for a while, and I just hadn't noticed.

Either way, once I realized just how much communication with my husband consisted of grunting, it was hard *not* to notice.

Time to take out the trash? Grunt. Reminders about doctor's appointments? Grunt. Saying goodnight? *Grunt*.

I push the eggs around my plate with a fork. Maybe this is simply what happens to every marriage after decades together—you spend so much time in each other's presence that your brains revert back to cavemen speech.

With thirty-four years together, we've certainly clocked in the hours. We met just after college, which I'm reminded of by Larry's choice of t-shirt today.

It's his red one, with his college mascot on it—only Larry fills it out now a lot more than he did back then. I've been sitting across from that shirt at this table for almost three and half decades now.

As I scoop another forkful of eggs into my mouth, I find myself thinking of how it used to be between us, back when we were first married.

We could hardly keep our hands off each other. Every second apart felt like a lifetime. Sometimes, we couldn't wait until Friday nights to see each other.

A smile touches my face as I think about the bathroom in Larry's first apartment—the only place we could go for some privacy, considering he shared a room with two other guys.

I snake my hand across the table and cup his, my fingertips running over the small wiry hairs on his knuckles. The newspaper comes down a few inches, allowing Larry's eyes to meet mine.

I smile and give his hand a squeeze. "Want to go into the bathroom for a minute?"

"What for? Is something broken? I'll call Jimmy first thing," Larry says, his head darting to the left to get a look at the first-floor bathroom.

Quickly I shake my head, my hand retreating back over the tabletop. "No, nothing's broken... never mind."

Larry lets out a breath and lifts his newspaper again, speaking from behind its papery barricade.

"Okay, good. Scared me for a second... that piping on the side is shoddy, I just know it. Only a matter of time until it goes."

I nod silently, twisting my hands together in my lap. And just like that, we're back to the silence.

The kitchen is quiet around me, apart from the fading wail of the firetruck as it drives out of hearing distance.

It feels like every morning has become the same. Even more so now that it's summer, and school is out.

Back when I had to go in, at least I had the commute and the kids to break up the monotony. For the next couple of months however, there isn't going to be any of that.

My stomach tightens a little as I think of teaching. I'm still not entirely decided on what I'm going to do about the upcoming school year.

The sun beats down outside, baking the sidewalk beyond our gate. The dark asphalt of the street beyond that looks like it's practically liquid.

Another scorcher today, that's for sure. In a few minutes Larry will head off to work, and then I'll be alone in this house.

His arm comes up as he glances at his watch, and then he grunts again.

"Better get going."

He pushes away from the table, the chair scraping against the tile floor. His work uniform shirt hangs on the back of his chair, and he slips it on over his t-shirt.

Larry starts toward me, and my heart beats a little faster—a kiss goodbye—but then he reaches behind me to pluck his hat from its knob on the wall.

He runs a hand through his thinning hair to straighten it before pulling on the ballcap. Giving his watch another check, he grabs his lunchbox from the kitchen counter.

My eyes hang on the lunchbox for a moment. I'm thinking about how long it's been since he's met me for lunch at the school.

Years ago, I'd spot him through the chain link fence around the schoolyard, coming to me with that lunchbox in one hand and a bundle of flowers in the other.

I can't remember the last time he did that.

"Alright, I'm gonna get going. Try to stay cool in this heat. Love you," Larry says as he heads down the hallway to the front door.

"Love you too," I say, still staring at the counter where the lunchbox sat.

The words are flat, empty. I hear the squealing spring of the front screen door as he pushes it open, and then the bang as it claps shut again.

How did this happen? How did our loving marriage fade to the point that we're basically nothing more than roommates? I pick at a bump on the wooden tabletop with a fingernail.

The open window lets in waves of hot air that already have my skin slick with sweat, though it's early.

The simple solution would be to just crank up the air conditioning, but that would spike our electric bill so high we'd both have a heart attack.

Between my teaching salary and Larry's MTA mechanic position, we certainly aren't rolling in it. The last thing we need is higher bills.

I think of Larry again, his back as he left the house without a glance over his shoulder, and this routine we've fallen into, and something inside of me stirs.

It's just a flurry of a feeling, like the sudden quickening of your heart when you see a mouse dart across the floor, but it feels like a precursor to something bigger. Something you can't fix with a bit of cheese and a spring.

If we keep going like this, I'm not sure I'll be able to take it. More of the same, day in and day out.

Something needs to change.

We need a break from the monotony, a switch-up. A vacation from everyday life.

A chance to find *us* again.

But with money as tight as it is, a vacation to paradise isn't happening.

I stop picking at the table as a thought pops into my head.

Yes, something definitely needs to change, and I think I might know how to make it happen.

TWO

It's perfect.

I settle down in front of the computer in the study, my hands buzzing with so much excitement I can hardly press the power button to fire up Larry's laptop.

Marlene mentioned last time I saw her that she and the kids used this house-swapping website to escape the city for a week, and for no cost at all.

Basically, you trade houses with someone else for a period of time.

She showed me the pictures of this adorable little cottage out on Cape Cod, something that would've been hundreds of dollars if not thousands to rent for the time they stayed.

But since the owners of the cottage were looking for an affordable place to stay in the city, it was a win for both sides.

While Astoria, Queens isn't quite as trendy as Brooklyn, where Marlene lives, maybe Larry and I can find someone who'd be interested in swapping for our place.

After all, we do have a view of the Manhattan skyline at the end of our street. That's got to count for something, right?

The computer whirrs to life, the fan inside it letting out a rising whine as the old system boots up. Add a new computer to the long list of things we need and can't afford.

Grabbing hold of the mouse, I wave it around a moment to find my cursor before navigating to the search bar. The website for house-trading was called SwapN-Stay.com, if my memory serves.

I type that in and eagerly wait for the page to load. This could be exactly what Larry and I need—a little time away from it all, just the two of us.

A chance for us to really reconnect again.

The website finally loads, and I scroll through the home page, reading about how the process works.

To exchange houses, you have to upload pictures of your house and then "like" other houses you might like to trade with. If the other owner feels the same way, then you can begin messaging and ironing out the details.

The next couple hours speed by as I tidy up the place as best I can for the photos. I definitely want to show the place in the best light possible.

Beads of sweat pop up along my hairline as I work, the house temperature rising as the sun gets higher and higher overhead.

Out in the street, I hear a couple of children screaming as they play.

Straightening back up, I take a moment to catch my

breath and observe my handiwork. The place really doesn't look half-bad, at least to me.

Hopefully someone else thinks so, too.

I take a few photos of the house interior and then step outside to get a shot of the exterior and the city skyline as well.

With the blue sky as we have today and no rain expected, the buildings are crystal clear in the distance. They practically sparkle as the sun spotlights them.

Hurrying back inside, I begin the process of uploading the photos. Once that's done, I scroll down the website form and fill out the small box describing how long we're looking to be gone for.

A week sounds about right. Larry should have enough vacation days for that.

.Then it's time for the exciting part, searching through the other houses available on the site. Right away I filter by location. I'm definitely looking for something coastal, a place where we can escape this city heat.

After clicking through a few places, I pause on a cottage on Long Island. *Cottage* really doesn't do it justice —mansion would be a better descriptor.

The home is absolutely stunning. Large windows face the open ocean, providing a practically unobstructed view of the sea just beyond a green yard that quickly turns into a beach.

Everything inside looks brand new, shiny stovetop and counters and airy rooms.

Why would someone ever want to leave a place like this?

Even though there's a zero percent chance whoever

owns this gorgeous home would ever want to stay in a dumpy two-bedroom townhouse in Queens, I give the place a like anyway.

Can't hurt to try, right?

I sift through a few more listings, liking pretty much anything that would put us within walking distance of the beach and cooling ocean breezes. Just thinking about it makes me smile.

Before I know it, it's mid-afternoon and I'm starving. I make myself lunch and wipe the beads of sweat from my brow with a paper towel.

Soon enough Larry will be home. I consider telling him my idea for a getaway but then decide not to. I'm not sure why exactly—maybe I just need to be sure we actually have somewhere to go first.

As much as I want to sit by the computer and refresh the screen, hoping for any likes on our house, I know I need to give it some time.

Settling onto the couch, I dive into a psychological thriller by my favorite author, Freida McFadden.

The sound of bootsteps and the jingle of keys tell me that Larry is home again.

Pulling open the shades, I just manage to catch the back of him as he steps through the doorway and comes inside.

He lets out a cough as he shuffles down the hall, appearing at the entrance to the living room a moment later.

"Heat just won't quit. Nearly passed out in the tunnels today," he says.

There are streaks of grease on his hands from

working on the subway cars. He smears them across the front of his pants.

"It's definitely a scorcher," I agree. "I kicked the AC on a couple hours ago. Just couldn't stand it anymore."

Larry looks up sharply at that.

"Only a couple hours," I assure him.

He breathes out. "Okay. How was your day?"

Should I tell him my plan now?

No, I won't. Not yet. It's not even a plan, really, not until we've got somewhere to go.

"Good."

"Good. That's good," Larry replies.

We look at each other in silence for a moment. Larry coughs again.

"Want to watch something?" I ask.

"Was gonna watch the game," Larry says.

"Oh. Okay."

Then he's walking down the hallway and into the kitchen, where I hear him pull open the fridge for a beer.

"I'll be downstairs," he shouts through the house.

His boots thud on the basement steps as he descends.

Downstairs is his "man cave" as he likes to call it, where he's got a recliner set up in front of a large flat screen to watch any and all sports on TV.

This time of year, I don't even know what's on, but Larry always seems to find something he wants to watch.

Usually he doesn't head down for a couple hours after getting home. Given the heat though, I suppose it makes sense as the basement *is* the coolest place in the house.

I get up and go to the kitchen to start working on

dinner. Outside, the waning sun finally relents its onslaught of punishing heat.

The sky visible through the kitchen window is a mixture of blue and pink. I can't help but imagine what this sunset would look like from a beach, wide open and unobstructed.

A shout from Larry comes up from the basement. I guess his team did something well. How is it that he communicates more with that television than his wife?

Once dinner is ready, I walk over to the basement door and pull it open.

"Dinner is on the table," I shout down.

"Thanks hon," Larry says back.

The noise from the TV shuts off as Larry appears at the bottom of the staircase.

There aren't any sounds besides the clinking of our silverware off the plates as we cut into the chicken. I can't stand it anymore and speak up.

"So, it was a good day at work today?" I ask.

Larry swallows and nods. "Good, yeah... it was good. Hot but good. How was yours?"

"Good. Dr. Richards called, he wanted to know if the seventh still works."

Larry takes a sip of his beer and then nods. "Should. I'll call him tomorrow."

I nod and put another bite of chicken into my mouth as we return to the clanking.

After dinner, it's time to start the nightly routine. I go into the bathroom first, washing my face and brushing my teeth before heading down the hallway and into the bedroom.

Larry lets out a hacking cough and spits into the sink as he brushes his teeth, the rushing water from the faucet doing little to cover up the sound. I turn over in bed, studying the wallpaper for a moment before pushing off the covers.

I won't be able to sleep until I at least check the house swap website. I know it's been less than a day, but I just have to check. Larry gurgles and spits as I open the door to the spare room and sit down in front of the laptop.

As usual, it doesn't fire up immediately. My foot taps absentmindedly, my gaze drifting to the window to my left that allows me a view of the quiet street outside.

I can just make out the tops of the tallest skyscrapers in the distance. In Manhattan, the night is probably buzzing with activity.

The only buzzing I hear is Larry's electric toothbrush.

The screen glows to life, and I tap in the website address. After a few seconds of buffering, the page finally loads.

My eyes are pulled immediately to the inbox at the top right corner, where a glowing dot of orange alerts me to the fact that I have a match.

My heart beats like hummingbird wings as I navigate to the inbox and click on it.

I can't believe we've already got a match. The page buffers again, but when it finally loads, I'm left staring with my mouth hanging open.

We matched with the seaside cottage on Long Island.

The nicest home on this website, by far. And they

chose *us*. The hummingbird is now darting all around my chest.

I blink, but the match is still there on the screen when I open my eyes. Not a mirage. I let out a scoff, the corners of my mouth turning up into a smile.

Unbelievable. Whoever owns the gorgeous estate on the ocean wants to stay *here*.

It's almost too good to be true, but no, it says right there: *You have a match.*

For a moment I wonder again why someone with a place that nice would ever want to leave, especially in Summer.

In the house's description, it says: *Must be comfortable staying in an old house. Harder than it seems!*

I chuckle. This place is absolutely stunning. How bad can it be?

THREE

I can't stop staring at the screen, my chest fluttering with excitement as the hummingbird has invited some friends.

We've matched.

We might really be able to do this thing.

Visions of Larry and I walking hand-in-hand down the beach while the sun sets behind us move across my mind. Our beach chairs facing the waves, toes in the sand.

This isn't just a hope anymore—this can really happen.

Larry shuffles down the hallway to the bedroom, clearing his throat. I turn off the computer and join him in the bedroom, the two of us readying ourselves for bed on opposite sides of the room.

It's hard to contain my excitement, but now doesn't feel like the right time to tell him about it. He's always a little grouchy before bed, having been on his feet all day.

I glance over at my husband, but it's almost like he's

forgotten I'm even here in the room with him as he pulls on his sleep shirt, facing away from me.

No words are exchanged as we get ready for bed in silence.

It's quiet. Routine. We are beside each other, but not *with* each other.

"Goodnight," I say to Larry as we crawl under the covers.

"Goodnight, hon."

We do our usual kiss goodnight and then turn off the lights. I find myself staring up at the dark ceiling, my hands clasped on my stomach as Larry rolls over onto his side, facing away from me.

A weeklong vacation in the most beautiful home I've ever seen. Just Larry and me. A chance to rekindle our marriage.

This will be exactly what we need.

MY HANDS BUZZ as I land in front of the computer the next day.

I could hardly keep myself contained all morning, unable to think of anything but the house match waiting for me. Larry's off to work, and when he comes home tonight, I'll have everything planned out and ready.

The website loads, and then I click over to the matches again.

It's still there, I didn't dream it. I open up the messaging system that allows me to communicate with the other homeowners.

The owner of the cottage is named Kevin P. There's a small profile picture beside his name that shows a smiling man with brown hair parted neatly on the side, sporting glasses.

He appears to be about my age, maybe a few years younger. My fingers hover over the keyboard as I rack my brain.

What to say?

I don't know why I feel so nervous—I guess I just don't want anything to mess this up. My heart pounds faster as I settle on a message and begin to type it out.

Hello Kevin, I'm Debra. You have a wonderful home, I type.

To my complete surprise, I see a bubble pop up that lets me know Kevin is online and typing his response. My heart pounds against my sternum again.

Thanks Debra, and same to you, he replies.

The bubbles pop up again, meaning he's sending another message.

It says you're looking to stay for about a week? Kevin asks.

Yes, I type, *we'd love to just get out of the city for a little while.*

Well that works out beautifully, because I'm looking to get out of Long Island for a while, too.

I shake my head. *Why would anyone ever want to leave the beach?*

Haha, Kevin types, *That's usually true. My wife and I just separated, and I can't stay here anymore. It reminds me too much of her.*

I'm very sorry to hear that, I type.

Thank you. I could use a distraction, and I can't think of a better one than NYC.

My throat tightens a little. He knows this house is in Queens, right? The nearest subway stop is a fifteen-minute walk away. Not exactly Times Square.

As much as I want to go ahead with this, I don't want him to get the wrong idea about where we are.

I live in Queens, I type, *so it takes a little while to get into Manhattan. Just so there's no confusion.*

Kevin's typing bubble appears again.

Yes, I saw that. I think that's perfect, because I can get a taste of downtown but also have some peace and quiet when I need it, he writes.

A smile breaks out across my face. Fantastic. Even though I've never really thought so, I suppose our house really is in a pretty good "best of both worlds" spot for city life.

Now, it truly is a win-win.

The next step is figuring out when we actually want to go through with this exchange.

Kevin types that he is ready to swap at any time, which is understandable. I don't think I'd like to spend all day in a house that reminded me of my ex, either.

His message waits on the screen for my response.

When can you come?

I sit back at the desk to think. There really isn't any reason we couldn't leave soon, save for Larry's job. But even then, he's got plenty of vacation days saved, seeing as he never uses them.

What's stopping us from leaving this weekend?

In fact, I think we should. Why wait around, doing

the same thing for another week? I want to work on things now, try to fix us now.

Another week of grunting might just do me in.

My fingers hit the keyboard as I type out my response, a smile on my face.

Is this weekend too soon?

That works for me! Kevin writes in reply.

Great!

I let out a little breath, my heart fluttering. Okay then. It's settled. This weekend, we head for Long Island. I'll just have to convince Larry once he gets home from work.

Just as I'm about to push away from the computer, I see that the text bubbles have popped up again. Kevin's typing out another message, so I settle back down and wait for it to come through.

It takes a few minutes, which tells me it's a long one.

Super excited to initiate this house exchange. I think it'll be a really good thing for both of us. Just a few things I'd like to make you aware of before your stay.

The house... while beautiful, definitely has its quirks. Part of the charm in living in an old farmhouse, after all. I've gotten used to them over the years, but for someone else, it might take a little getting used to.

For instance, there's a lot of odd sounds at night. And by odd, I mean sometimes downright spooky. You might start to think there's someone else in the home with you, but I assure you, it's just the house's old bones settling. Nothing to be concerned about, I promise.

Another thing—the doors might also be a little creaky. They might even open on their own. Another part of older house charms. Warped, old wood. Again, nothing to be too worried over.

While a little strange at first, I'm sure you, like I have, will learn to really love this place during the time you're here. In fact, I can practically guarantee it.

Feel free to use any and all silverware, plates, and glasses. Towels and fresh sheets are in the upstairs closet. I think I've got a few bottles of wine tucked away as well, if that's of any interest.

In terms of outdoor activities, I've got beach chairs, kayaks, and a beach umbrella on the porch. Please utilize those at your leisure. Basically, what's mine is yours. The bedrooms, the TV, the Adirondack chairs—feel free to use whatever you like.

I shake my head in wonder. How incredible is this?

It's turning into an all expenses paid vacation, alcohol included. I reach forward to start typing out my thanks, only to see the text bubbles reappear again.

One last message from Kevin.

Really, there's only one rule—don't go downstairs into the basement.

FOUR

Larry arrives a few minutes after six, letting out a sigh as he shuts the door.

"AC went out in the car today," he calls from the hallway. He sounds tired.

I hear him drop his lunchbox as he lowers himself to the chair beside the door to start untying his work boots.

I'm so full of excitement I can't wait for him to finish. Pushing up from my armchair, I go to meet him in the front hallway.

Larry glances up at me, clearly a little surprised at this break in routine.

"How was your day?" he asks, his fingers tugging at the knot of his boot laces.

"I've got some news," I say, my heart beating faster.

Larry's face pales. "What's wrong? Who died?"

Quickly I shake my head. Why is *news* always considered to be negative?

"No one died. We're going on vacation," I say.

He blinks. "We are?"

I nod, biting my lip. I wasn't sure what kind of reaction I was expecting, but Larry doesn't look as enthused as I would've hoped.

Then he gives a shake of his head. "You know how tight money is, hon. We can't just—"

"It's free, totally free," I say, cutting him off.

"I signed us up for this house exchange website, the one Marlene told me about. Anyway, there's someone out on Long Island who's agreed to switch with us. The house is adorable, Larry—and right on the beach."

He's silent for a moment. Then his face contracts, screwing up in a scowl.

"Wait, house...exchange? So there's gonna be some random people staying in our home?" he asks. "I don't know about that. I really wish you would've checked with me first."

He stands, still frowning as he looks down at me.

I cross my arms. "It's just one person. And I didn't check with you because I figured you'd say no before you even saw the homes that were available."

Larry's eyebrows shoot up. He can't argue. He knows I'm right.

"I just don't think..."

"You always say no, Larry," I say, the words rushing out of me suddenly.

"I don't always say no."

"When was the last time we did something?" I ask. "I mean outside of what we do every day, day in and day out. When was the last time we had *fun* together?"

My voice sounds a little more strained than I mean it to, and I think Larry notices it. My question sinks in for a moment before his mouth comes open and then closes again.

I surge forward, grabbing his hands in mine as the words start spilling out of me in a rush.

"Remember how spontaneous we used to be? People would always have trouble getting in contact with us because we'd be in a different country on a whim. It was always something new, something fun. What happened to that?"

I can see him thinking as I talk.

"We aren't twenty-five anymore, Debra," he says.

Taking a step forward, I wrap my arms around him and press my cheek to his chest.

"I miss that spontaneity, Larry. I miss *you*," I say quietly.

Larry hugs me in return. It feels good.

After a few seconds his hands wrap around my shoulders, and he sets me back so we can look at each other. His eyes search mine.

I take his callused hands again and squeeze, feeling something akin to a spark in my fingertips.

It's the most intimate we've been in who knows how long. After another moment of deliberation, Larry opens his mouth.

"Free, you said?" he asks.

A grin breaks out across my face, and I nod rapidly.

"A whole week in a cottage on the beach, completely free of charge. There's even complimentary wine."

"Okay then."

I pull him into another hug, squeezing him tight. For

a moment there, I truly thought Larry was ready to give up on this marriage altogether.

He might not have known it, but his decision to say yes wasn't just determining whether we'd go on the trip or not.

For me, there was a whole lot more riding on that answer.

"Thank you," I say, my eyes still shut tight as we embrace. "Thank you."

"I've got all those vacation days just burning a hole in my pocket anyhow," Larry says as we separate.

"Not sure what I've even been saving them for. More doctor trips, I suppose," he adds.

"Well now you get to spend them on fun," I say, rubbing a hand across my cheek.

That wasn't an actual tear that just eeked out of my eye, was it?

Larry sits on the bench again and goes back to work untying his boots.

"When is this house exchange happening?" he asks.

I walk toward the kitchen to get started on dinner. "This weekend."

There's a creak from Larry's chair as he straightens back up.

"This weekend? I don't know, there's talk of a potential storm brewing along the East Coast, isn't there?"

He wisely stops talking after the look I give him. It's now or never for us. I just can't keep going on like this otherwise, and it looks like Larry might finally be catching on to that.

"I'll let work know," he says.

I nod and then pull open the fridge, doing a little jog in place. I just can't keep still.

This is really happening.

I bite my lip and try to contain my excitement, anticipating what is sure to be a week filled with sun, sand, and rejuvenating relaxation.

FIVE

Coastal Long Island is like someone snuck into my wildest dreams and made them reality.

Everywhere we look, the most stunning homes I've ever seen lay scattered left and right, their yards decorated by flowerbeds and shrubs and luscious trees.

The ocean is a wallpaper of deep blue just beyond.

It takes us some time to navigate through the adorable town center, complete with brick facades and antique lampposts. I'm already in love with the area and feeling giddy, despite the light cloud layer that has overtaken the sky.

No amount of overcast could ever dampen this sense of joy I'm feeling.

Larry licks his lips and then turns the wheel to the left, the car letting out a loud squeal as we make a turn, following the driving directions from the house swap form.

As we pull away from the town, the houses seem to be getting bigger and bigger. Luscious yards roll outward like green carpets as we pass beautiful home after beautiful home.

We're moving down the street at a pretty good pace, but I'm still able to catch sight of a person as they round the side of their house carrying a sheet of plywood just before we fly by.

We turn onto another road, this one even quieter than the last. Large trees overhang their branches across the road like soldiers lining a royal walkway.

Larry eases his foot off the gas pedal to slow as we both look at the house numbers.

There's a large yellow house with white shutters to my left. It has the most magnificent garden full of blue and pink hydrangea flowers.

We drive past it and come upon a gravel driveway bordered on both sides by lush hedges about waist-height.

Larry leans forward until his nose is practically touching the windshield.

"Is this it?"

There's no house visible from here, but the driveway slopes gently down toward the blue ocean beyond.

Around us, the street is quiet. Birds chirp happily overhead, soaring across a sky filled with a spatter of clouds.

"I really, really hope so," I say, my heart beating a little faster.

I printed out Kevin's address so we'd have it here with us in the car. Reaching down, I unfold the paper and double-check the number.

Thirteen. A quick glance to our left, and I spot the

numbers that have been carved into the rock just beside the hedge. A one and a three. This is it.

I nod quickly, folding the paper once more as I shift in my seat.

"Yep. This is us," I say.

Even Larry seems excited, his lips splitting in a wide smile as we turn into the driveway entrance and start down the gravel lane. The tires take a moment to grip onto the white rocks, but then we are rolling down the slight hill and are greeted with a view that is absolutely breathtaking.

There's the house, even more beautiful than it appeared in the photos, which I wouldn't have thought possible.

It's two stories, built in a farmhouse style and adorned with a wrap-around porch and neatly manicured shrubs and flowers all blooming brightly.

That isn't even the best part, though. It's the near-one-hundred-and-eighty degree view of the ocean beyond, as blue as a sapphire gemstone.

"Wow," Larry says as we continue rolling down toward the gorgeous house.

The amazement is clear in his voice. Reaching over, I give his arm a squeeze.

This place is *ours* for the whole entire week.

The car squeals to a stop at the end of the driveway, the house just off to our left.

To my right is the yellow house, which is somehow just as attractive from the side as it was from the street.

From our new vantage point, I can see just how many back windows the place has, all with jaw-dropping views of the ocean right in their backyard. Smart builders, that's for sure.

Larry turns off the car and pockets the keys, a smile on his face.

"This is pretty incredible, Deb," he says as he gets out and stretches.

I beam at that. "Thanks."

Larry goes to the trunk to pull out our suitcases. "I'll take these inside. You go take a look around."

Strolling across the yard, I take another long look at the ocean, stretching my arms out to the side as I enjoy the fantastic breeze. I feel like spinning around in a circle like a child.

I can't believe this is going to be my view for the next seven days.

Beats looking at Mrs. Washington's damp laundry swaying in the breeze, that's for sure.

The suitcases hit the gravel, and Larry lets out a grunt as he tugs them toward the front door.

"Kevin said the key is under the rock by the hydrangeas," I call over to him.

He nods, his muscles flexing as he jerks the suitcases across the uneven surface of the gravel driveway.

Reaching the stone walkway, he drags them with considerably more ease up to the front porch steps. I see him bend down beside the hydrangea rock, remaining bent for another second before straightening.

"Found it," he says, holding up the key.

I cross the yard again and round the front of the car to follow after him.

It feels like my head is on a swivel as I try to take in

every single detail of our new surroundings. It's hard to look away because it's all so wonderful.

As soon as we get settled, I'm going to send Kevin another message telling him just how grateful we are to be here. I feel light, bubbly. This is beyond perfect.

Larry gets the front door unlocked, and it swings inward, revealing the absolutely adorable interior of the home.

We've got plenty of our own ocean-facing windows, which stretch across the entire back of the house, letting light fill the space. The placement of them almost gives the illusion that the house is sitting on top of the ocean.

Larry pushes the suitcases to the side and plants his hands on his hips as he turns side to side and surveys the layout of the house.

He lets out a low whistle. "Are you kidding me? What does this guy do for a living?"

Directly in front of us is the staircase that leads up to the second floor, with a large living room area off to our left. Beyond that is the screened-in porch and then the back deck, complete with its very own Adirondack chairs and fire pit.

We move from room to room, little gasps escaping my mouth as I go. I just can't believe all of this is actually ours for the week. I feel like a lottery winner or something.

The kitchen features a large marble-topped island, a woven basket atop it with a bottle of wine from Kevin. Larry grunts his approval at that as I glide my hand across the cool marble countertop, pausing at the large appointment calendar beside the fridge.

It's a little nosy, yes, but I can't help but glance over it. Looks like Kevin is a busy man.

"Wow," I say, pointing at one appointment in particular. "Look at this one. *Dr. DeLuca here, 3 PM.* How well off do you have to be for a doctor to make house calls?"

"Or how messed up," Larry adds with a shrug.

I scoff. We move through the kitchen into the dining room and then make our way back toward the front of the house where we left our suitcases.

Larry nods, taking it all in.

"Well, it's quite a place. But where's the bathroom?" he asks after another moment.

He takes a couple steps forward, passing by a large ornate mirror hanging in the entryway as he makes his way to the door below the staircase. I'm still entranced by the interior, my neck craning as I look up at the large antique chandelier hanging from the ceiling far above us.

The jiggling of the doorknob gets my attention. The door begins to swing open.

"Wait," I say, "That's got to be the door to the basement," I say, remembering Kevin's message.

"He said that's the one area that's off-limits."

Larry looks back at me. "Probably should've locked it then. I wonder what he's got down there that's so important we can't go in there."

"Private stuff, I'm sure," I say, grabbing hold of my suitcase handle.

Larry remains at the basement door another second.

"House rules, Lar. Come on, let's get settled in," I say. "There'll be a bathroom upstairs. Probably a whole bunch of them."

He turns away from the door and joins me in the foyer, grabbing hold of his own suitcase and then heading for the staircase. Its steps are wide and slightly shorter than I'm used to, but I adjust quickly because it's actually easier to ascend than ours back home.

Lining the wall beside us are ornamental picture frames, though four of them are completely empty, showcasing nothing more than the beautiful wood paneled wall behind them.

"What's the deal with that?" Larry grunts, nudging his chin at one empty frame as we step past it.

"Kevin's going through a divorce, remember?" I say.

I'm sure the frames once held pictures of the wife he no longer has, so I don't exactly blame him.

The pictures that remain are photographs of the ocean, flowers, boats. All beautiful, but not enough to completely even out the glaring holes in the whole display. The result is a melancholy sense of something missing, of incomplete-ness.

We reach the second floor landing and drop our suitcases, only huffing a little. There's a blue and white hallway rug up here that leads us down toward the main bedroom, passing a bathroom and two closets.

I let out a little gasp as we step inside the bedroom.

Nearly the entire back wall is glass. The floor to ceiling windows and set of French doors show a balcony on the other side... and chairs that face the ocean.

Pretty much my dream come true.

One of the windows beside the doors is slightly open, allowing a light breeze to lift the pale sea-green curtains.

They flutter almost as if they were alive, nearly reaching the edge of the desk beside the bed.

The bed itself is a king and sports a comforter with a nautical navy pattern and matching pillow shams with a generous array of coral-colored throw pillows.

Larry pushes his suitcase to the side and heads for the doors to the balcony.

He throws the lock, and then pulls them open to allow in a whoosh of salty air that washes over us like a cooling ocean wave.

"Not bad at all," he says approvingly.

"See? I knew you'd love it," I say, coming up beside him.

I lower my head to his shoulder, my temple resting against his arm as we stand there for a few moments. He doesn't move away. My heart soars.

We remain like that for another few seconds until Larry clears his throat.

"I really do need to use the bathroom."

We separate, and he shuffles off toward the door to the en suite bathroom.

"Where's my camera? I want to get some photos of this for Marlene to see," I ask.

"I put it in the small suitcase," Larry says over his shoulder.

I look around the room for a moment then remember the smaller bag is still sitting on the backseat of the car.

"I'm gonna go grab it," I tell Larry, who nods and then pulls the bathroom door shut behind him.

The muffled sounds of him clearing his throat follow me as I head back down the stairs and land on the first floor again. Stepping onto the front porch, I get another look up at the sky, which seems slightly more gray than before.

Hm. I was hoping the cloud layer would burn off, but that doesn't look like it'll be the case today.

Oh well. The beach is just as beautiful on a cloudy day in my eyes.

I step off the porch and start down the walkway back toward the car.

"Hello?"

I lift my head and look around to see a woman standing by the hedges separating our house from the yellow one. She's wearing a pair of gardening gloves and a wide-brimmed sun hat.

"Hi," I say, giving her a little wave.

She doesn't move, which strikes me as a little odd. Instead, she's just standing there, still staring at me with her sunglasses on.

I look down again, trying to pretend like I'm not paying any attention to her as I walk to the car and open the back door. My pulse thuds in my ears as I glance back over at her to find her *still* standing there.

Why is she still staring?

I drop my hands and stare back at her, holding her gaze.

"Can I help you with something?" I ask.

The woman's eyebrows push together.

"Who are you? What are you doing here?" she asks.

Why is she acting like this is so strange? With the popularity of online home-booking websites these days, it's not exactly a novel concept.

"Debra Walsh. We rented this place for the week,"
I say.

Even though she's wearing sunglasses, I can tell the
woman's eyes widen at my words as her brows raise above
the rims.

When she speaks again, the note of disbelief in her
voice is palpable.

"You're staying *there*?"

SIX

I'm taken aback by her reaction.

The way she said it, you would've thought there was a condemned building behind me, not a gorgeous cottage with a panoramic ocean view.

"Yes... it's me and my husband staying here. Why?" I ask her.

The woman shakes her head slightly, seemingly having recovered from her initial shock.

"I see, sorry. It's probably... nevermind," the woman says, taking a step back from the hedge.

Now I'm intrigued, though. This woman's eyes just about fell out of her head when she heard we were going to be staying here, and of course I want to know why.

"Wait a minute," I say, stepping around the car, forgetting the suitcase for the moment.

The woman is already a few paces back from the hedge line, seeming like she wants to leave in a hurry.

"Hey," I call after her. She pauses.

"Why were you so surprised we were staying here?"

The woman seems almost as if she is debating something, and then her shoulders drop. She takes a couple of steps back toward me and the hedge.

When she speaks again, her voice is much quieter.

"That house you're staying in... it just... wasn't a happy home, okay?" she says.

Her voice is barely above a whisper, even though it's just us here. I stare at her for a moment, trying to understand.

"The separation," I offer up. "Kevin mentioned that. He—"

"The talk around town is there was no separation at all," the woman says quickly, cutting me off.

I blink. "What? What do you mean?"

The neighbor gives me a pointed look.

"Even living right next door, we barely saw them," she says. "The Petersons, I mean. But every once in a while, when the wind moved a certain way... we could hear the arguing. And then about a week ago, right when they *separated*... well we haven't seen them since. Him... or *her*."

My chest tightens as I work through the woman's words. Despite the warm temperature, I can't help but feel like I'm suddenly a few degrees cooler.

"There's just a lot of questions going around," the woman finishes.

This is a lot of information being thrown at me at once. *Is* it information, though, really? Or just small town rumors, bored housewife talk that's been exaggerated each time it's told?

"And you are?" I ask.

"Cheryl. Miller," Cheryl says, extending a gloved hand over the hedge.

I shake it.

"Well, we were just inside. Everything seems completely normal," I say, working to keep my voice even.

Cheryl nods quickly. "Right, sure. I'm sure it's all a bunch of hoopla anyhow. You know how it can get in places like this—any drama is suddenly anyone's business. Really what we should be more concerned about is this storm."

I had turned my head to look toward the street at a passing car, but snap my attention back to her. Larry mentioned something about a possible storm too.

After looking into it, I concluded it wasn't going to amount to anything serious. But that was last night's news. Has something changed?

"Storm?" I ask, feeling my chest tighten a little.

Cheryl nods again. As she does, I look past her to the piles of aluminum sheets leaning against the side of her house.

Is she boarding up the windows? People only do that when it's a really big storm.

"Wanted to make sure the storm panels were still good from last season," she says.

"I thought it wasn't supposed to be serious," I say, concerned now.

"You live by the water long enough, you learn to take all storms seriously," Cheryl says with a nod.

"Forecast looks okay for now, but how well can we really know Mother Nature? Things can turn on a dime out here on the island. We haven't had a real bad one in a while, feels like we're due. Cons of living right on the ocean, I suppose."

I glance back up at the sky. Somehow, it seems even darker than when I stepped outside five minutes ago. What had been nothing more than a thin layer of gray is now looking more and more swollen.

My stomach tightens, a result of all the new information I've just taken in, both about the weather and our hosts. None of it's great.

Fighting, arguments. Rumors something bad might've happened. As Cheryl steps away from the hedge again to continue her work, I force myself to take a deep breath.

That's all it is. Rumors. Delivered by a nosy neighbor with nothing better to do.

Besides, there are more pressing matters at hand, like the potential storm. What if it does hit?

Maybe Larry's cynicism had actually been right. I chew on my lip and glance up again as a small droplet of water lands on my forehead.

I let out a sigh and shut my eyes, mentally pushing back at the dark thoughts that have cropped up in my head.

This was supposed to be a week of relaxation and reconnection between me and my husband. That's starting to look less and less likely, but I'm not going to give up.

Maybe the storm won't be as bad as they're saying. A little rain here and there, but nothing more.

Either way, I can't go back home now. If I do, I'm not sure Larry and I will be going home together.

This is our chance to fix things, to find ourselves again as a couple, and I'm not giving up on that.

Maybe a week trapped inside with only each other is just what we need. Rain can be romantic at times.

Another drop splashes down on my hair as I go back to the car and retrieve the small suitcase from the back-seat. As I slam the door shut and hustle back toward the house, Cheryl's words about it echo through my mind.

It wasn't a happy home.

Still, she doesn't know the Petersons well—she said she hardly saw them. It's only rumors.

Right?

SEVEN

I open up Larry's laptop on my knees as the TV blares in front of me.

He's seated on the other end of the couch, eyes locked on the screen as the weatherman elaborates on the forecast for the coming days.

"—potential record levels of rainfall," the man says, gesturing behind him to a graphic of Long Island and New York City.

Almost all the land is covered by green, which symbolizes rain.

Larry shakes his head as he watches. "Knew it was too good to be true. Told you it was gonna storm."

I look over at him as the laptop whirs to life. Hot air is forced out of the vents on its sides and onto my knees as a light rain patters the windows.

"It's still a day out," I say. "The path can change, you know that. How many times did we hear *potential for record snowfall* in the city, and then wake up to find nothing more than a dusting?"

Larry only grunts in response, which irks me.

It feels like I had to move mountains to get us here, and now it seems like Larry is looking for any excuse to leave. Like he's ready to throw in the towel.

A gust of wind outside slings more drizzle against the windows. The sun has nearly set now, the sky almost completely dark.

As close as we are to the ocean, the wind is pretty strong here. The house creaks against the force of the gusts, making me glance up at the ceiling.

"...so we'll just have to wait and see," the weatherman finishes on the TV.

"We should go to the store tomorrow and get some flashlights and water," Larry says as he reaches for the remote.

I nod and then glance back down at the laptop as it comes to life in my lap.

The bright glow of the screen glares a little in the relative darkness of the living room, especially when the TV goes dark for a moment as Larry switches channels.

I type in the address of the house swap website and log in, finding a message already waiting for me.

Scrolling across the mousepad, I navigate to the inbox and open it.

Kevin: *Just arrived. Your house is exactly what I was looking for. This will be the perfect distraction! Everything okay on your end?*

I chew my lip between my teeth as I read over his message, the TV blaring behind me. Briefly, I consider asking for more information about his separation but then decide against it.

That's way too invasive a question for a person I don't even know. Besides, he's been nothing but cordial and generous with us so far, and I don't want to ruin anything before we've even gotten settled in here.

Everything is great! Found the key no problem. Hoping this storm misses us so we can make the most of the beach, I type in reply.

I saw that on the news, Kevin types. *Hopefully it's all overblown.*

Yes. Here's hoping, I close on a positive note.

I made sure to pack the beach cooler with some sandwich meat and a few microwaveable meals so that we'd have something until we could get to the grocery store. It's coming in handy tonight because neither of us is eager to get out and go shopping right now.

We're having hamburgers and peas, which I heat up on the stovetop while Larry watches whatever sports channel they have available here.

The wind presses against the windows as we sit down at the dinner table to eat. My fork clanks against the side of my plate as I scoop up some peas, chewing quietly.

Larry sits opposite me, his head turned to peer out the back windows at the darkness outside. No moon tonight to provide an ocean view.

"Sounds like the wind might be picking up," he says.

He turns back to me. "Should we just call it? A week of rain doesn't exactly sound like my kind of holiday."

I set down my fork and swallow. "You want to leave?"

"Don't you? What's the beach with no sun? This was a good idea, but maybe we should try again some other time," he says.

"Is it really about the weather... or do you just not want to be here with me?" I ask, my voice hardening a little.

Larry stops chewing. "What's that supposed to mean?"

"What I asked. Is it really about the weather? I'm not sure how it's going to be any better looking at rain through our windows at home instead of these," I say.

"Well..." Larry starts but doesn't really have anything decent to reply with.

He looks down at his plate and scoops up a forkful of peas. I look down at my own plate as the sound of the wind outside fills in the silence that has descended between us.

This isn't going as well as I'd hoped.

After dinner, we sit down in front of the television again. Larry clicks through the channels, surfing to see what's on. We pass by *The Holiday*, one of my favorite Christmas movies. A little too early in the year for that, though.

After mindlessly watching some disaster movie, it's time to get ready for bed. We both push off the couch and shuffle into the main hallway where the staircase is. Even though we're still a little frosty, I look over at Larry, seeking some sort of reconciliation.

He doesn't return my gaze. He's looking at the basement door.

I have to admit, I've looked at it a few times myself.

It sits there, unmoving in the dark house. Unlocked. In two seconds, we could be down there.

Questions about what could possibly be behind it crop up in my mind, but I shake them off.

Trudging up the stairs together, we take turns getting ready for bed in the bathroom. Afterward, I slide into bed beside Larry, who is little more than a lump under the sheets in the dark.

To our left are the French doors to the balcony, which creak with every gust of wind.

All those windows provide an amazing view during the daytime, but now that it's night, I can't help but feel a little overexposed.

Larry rolls over, murmuring to himself as he shifts position. I look up at the white painted boards of the ceiling, wide awake, running through our dinner conversation in my head.

This week of finding each other isn't exactly off to the best start.

Between the weather and the words we exchanged, I don't know if we're going to be able to do it. A flash of heat burns my stomach as my brain goes to worst-case scenarios.

I only allow that for a few seconds before managing to pull myself out of the doom spiral.

No, we have to try. Despite everything, we have to try.

Shutting my eyes, I try to focus on anything other than my marriage crumbling as sleep slowly overtakes me.

I don't seem to fully drop off though, not even after what feels like hours in bed. The wind, the rain, the unfamiliar bed all seem to keep me just inches above the surface of deep, restorative sleep.

Finally though, between imagined scenarios and fears, I can feel my body starting to slow. I've just—

Thump, thump.

My eyes snap open, my heart leaping up into my throat.

What was that?

Those were definite *thuds* from somewhere below us.

My pulse pounds in my ears, marking each passing second as I wait there in the dark. Sleep is far away now, my entire body feeling like a live wire as I remain stock-still in bed.

That didn't sound mechanical at all.

Larry has rolled over again beside me, his face pointing toward me now as he snores lightly. I glance over at him and then at the bedroom door. The rain taps at the glass beside us.

I swallow a breath of air. It was probably just the wind.

It's a stormy night, and this is an unfamiliar house. Kevin even mentioned that the house occasionally makes weird sounds.

I've got no idea how a house settles. Or what the plumbing is like in a place like this. Maybe that noise was just an old pipe.

I've very nearly convinced myself everything is fine when the unmistakable sound of a door shutting shatters any weak sense of comfort I might've had.

EIGHT

Larry's eyes open, his snore turning into a sharp intake of breath as he sits upright.

"What was that?" he asks.

"It came from downstairs," I whisper, the words coming out strangled.

That was most definitely a door closing.

Kevin might've mentioned weird house noises, and creaky doors, but he didn't say *anything* about doors shutting on their own.

There was an unmistakable creak, followed by a loud bang as it shut. Larry licks his lips beside me and hauls himself higher on the mattress. He's thinking what I'm thinking.

Someone is in the house.

Beside me, Larry's breath comes in short pants as the two of us stare at the bedroom door.

It's as if at any second now, someone is going to come smashing through the wood. I can hardly breathe my chest is so tight.

Almost as if on cue, the rain seems to pick up outside, slapping against the house with renewed vigor as we remain frozen in the darkness.

Larry glances to the side and then slides off the bed, his feet hitting the floor.

I whip my head over to him.

"What are you doing?" I hiss.

"I need to check it out, don't I?" he whispers back, digging his feet into his slippers.

My mouth opens, but nothing comes out. Larry shuffles across the bedroom and creeps to the door, which he slowly pulls open.

It lets out a low whine that has both of us sucking in a breath. I almost expect to hear shouting, maybe even pounding footsteps on the stairs—but there's nothing.

Just the rain outside and the wind that makes the house creak again. I get out of bed and follow Larry to the door. He's a few steps in front of me, his footsteps muffled by the carpet runner, as we head toward the staircase.

Just as we reach the second floor landing, I hear it again.

Thump, thump, thump.

Larry's body tenses like he's been struck by lightning. Out here in the hallway, the sound is even more clear.

It's definitely coming from somewhere below us, and it doesn't sound like any pipe I've ever heard.

Someone is down there.

My stomach is so wobbly I think I might vomit. There is someone in our house. Larry knows it too, his neck glistening with sweat in the weak glow of a hallway nightlight as he takes a shuddering breath.

Then to my absolute shock, he starts heading for the stairs.

"Larry," I hiss, "what are you doing?"

He glances back at me, eyes wide. "If someone's inside, I can't let them get you."

At the top of the staircase, he takes another breath and then cups his hands around his mouth.

"We know you're down there," he shouts, the volume of his voice making me jerk.

"The police are already on their way. I also have a gun, and train with it three times a week."

His words hang in the air as both of us wait with bated breath for a response. Shuffling, shouting?

My mind races, and my ears are so sensitive I could probably hear a single hair hitting the floor. I don't know where Larry came up with the line about a gun. He's never held one in his life.

Then my chest constricts at a new thought. What if *they* have a gun? An actual, real gun?

There's no response at all. The house continues to creak and shift with the wind and rain, but I don't hear any more thumping. After almost a solid minute of silence, Larry glances over at me and then slowly starts down the stairs.

I nearly chew through the skin on my lip as I watch him go. He keeps close to the bannister, gripping it hand-over-hand as he goes down in the dark.

He's only ten steps from the bottom now. Five. The wind whistles. Four.

Rain comes down outside. Three. The house lets out a hiss. Two. One.

Larry's on the first floor, a few feet from the front door. I'm wringing my hands so tightly I can hardly feel my fingers.

"Hello?" he shouts again.

I'm not sure what he plans to do if someone responds. He's got no weapon. He's wearing nothing but his boxers, sleep shirt, and slippers.

Turning to look behind him, Larry reaches over to something.

The entire space floods with light as the chandelier comes to life. It scalds my eyeballs, making me wince and stumble backward. I hear Larry performing a walk-through of the house below.

"No one's here," he says finally.

I step back up to the balcony railing and look down at him. My throat is dry.

His hands drop to his sides as he shakes his head. "Everything looks completely fine. All the windows and doors are still locked, nothing looks tampered with. It's just the house."

"What about the door?" I ask, "I know I heard one shut."

Larry steps away for a moment, and then I hear a door slam shut again. Footsteps, and then he reappears.

"This closet door, I think. One of us must've left it open when we were getting dinner ready. It must have shut," he says.

I try to rack my brain and remember if I left the door open or not. Between the early hour and my state of panic, I'm having trouble remembering what either of us did. Maybe he's right. I let out a shaky breath, unclenching my fists.

"It's an old house. There's a lot of wind outside," Larry says. "Some of it's gotta be getting in through the cracks and maybe between the walls. I'm sure under those conditions, the doors can open a little and shut again."

I give him a nod. Yes, that's got to be what we heard. We've gotten ourselves all worked up over nothing more than a storm and an old house doing what an old house does.

He lets out a breath and rubs his face, shaking his head. "Wow. That really had my blood pressure going."

Larry starts back up the staircase, letting out a yawn as he climbs.

"If one of us has a heart attack, can we sue Kevin P.?"

He reaches the top of the staircase and walks back down the hallway toward me.

"Come on. Let's go back to bed. It's the crack of dawn."

The two of us head into the bedroom, and my heart rate slowly begins to decrease. As Larry shuts the door and crawls back into bed, I find myself shaking my head.

Maybe I got so freaked out because of what Cheryl told me earlier. Her ominous words have me imagining all sorts of crazy things taking place in the dark.

Back in bed, everything slowly starts to become okay again. I even manage to salvage some sleep, drifting off to the gentle patter of the rain on the glass.

LIGHT ABOUNDS as we come down the stairs the next morning.

In the daylight, this place has a totally different vibe from last night. What just hours ago seemed ancient and foreboding today is quaint and charming.

The rain has stopped, too. In fact, as I step foot on the first floor, I'm delighted to see patches of blue sky between the clouds outside.

A smile grows across my face as I stride to the window and look out. There are a few branches strewn across the back lawn, but everything else looks okay. Another glance up reveals even more blue in the distance.

Maybe the worst of this system will miss us entirely. Still, it doesn't hurt to be prepared.

That's why we're making a trip into town this morning. I'll get us some groceries, and Larry will grab some extra flashlights, batteries and candles just in case.

With the way the weather is looking today, we might not even need them, but a little overpreparedness never killed anyone.

At worst, we'll have a healthy supply of AA batteries for the foreseeable future.

Larry pulls into a parking spot outside the grocery store and turns off the car.

"Okay, I'm going to head across the street to the hardware store. I'll meet you back here in an hour," he says.

"Sounds good," I say.

I've been thinking about something else too. Last night, when we thought someone was in the house, Larry stepped forward to defend me.

Said he couldn't let something happen to me.

Thinking of that warms my chest a little as we go our separate ways.

There's hope yet.

I start walking through the parking lot to the store entrance, heading in the direction of the steady flow of people going the same way. Looks like everyone else is stocking up, too.

Inside, I grab myself a shopping cart and follow the flow of people into the fruits and vegetables section. The cool refrigerated air makes me shiver as I direct the cart toward the apples.

If the weather does clear, I'd most definitely like to have a nice picnic on the beach.

"Mrs. Walsh?"

I lift my head, pulling my gaze from a bushel of apples to see who just said my name. It was a man's voice, and not one I recognize.

Turning to my left, I spot a tall man wearing a police uniform, his haircut short and neat.

He has a nice smile, and he's shaking his head side to side. "Wow, I can't believe it's you."

My eyebrows pull together. I really have no idea who this person is.

The man seems to sense this and smiles even wider. "Mrs. Walsh, It's Billy... Billy Ross. You taught me back in the city. Fourth grade."

As soon as he says the name, it's like a veil lifts, and I'm able to see his ten-year old face buried within his current manly one. It's so obvious now—those same mischievous eyebrows, the deep dimples as he grins.

"Oh my goodness, is that really you, Billy?" I say.

He comes forward, and we hug, drawing the curious eyes of a couple other shoppers near us.

"It's so great to see you," Billy says as we pull apart. "What are you doing on Long Island? Do you live here now?"

"Vacation," I say. "We're here for a week."

I haven't seen Billy since he was in fourth grade, but now that he's in front of me, it's like a rolodex of information about him has sprung back to mind. His parents were divorced, with his mother living in the city while his father stayed on Long Island.

Billy nods, still smiling. "Great, we're glad to have you. I moved back here after college—had enough of the city, you know? I always liked it more out here, anyway."

I'm smiling too. I'm just so flattered he's remembered me, even after two decades.

"And you're a police officer now," I say.

Billy's cheeks redden, exactly like they used to whenever he was slightly embarrassed as a little boy.

"I am. Just want to do my part," he says.

"Wonderful. That's wonderful," I say, nodding.

I chuckle. "I just can't believe you were able to recognize me. It's been so long."

Billy shakes his head. "I recognized you instantly. You haven't changed a bit, I don't think."

A snort escapes my mouth. "Now I *know* you're just being polite."

Billy smiles. "I mean it. You were always my favorite teacher, you know. I really appreciate what you did for me back then. With my parents' divorce and everything...

I wasn't in a good place. If you hadn't been so kind and encouraging of me, I'm not sure I'd be doing as well as I am today."

Now it's my turn to feel embarrassed.

"Oh Billy, that's awful nice of you to say, but I'm sure it wasn't just me," I say.

He shakes his head adamantly. "No, I mean it. You were there for me when it felt like no one else was."

I beam at that, feeling my eyes wet a little bit as we hug again. A pleasant warmth fills my chest as we embrace.

Little Billy Ross, all grown up.

"Where are you staying?" he asks.

"Oh, we're in a cottage on Water Lane," I say, giving him the address.

Billy nods. "Nice. That should be nice and quiet over there, most folks on Water skip town for Europe in August."

"And I'm more than happy to fill in for them," I say with a grin.

"Well, I'll let you get back to your shopping, Mrs. Walsh," Billy says, "but why don't we exchange numbers? You need anything while you're here, please don't hesitate to give me a call. I mean it."

We trade phone numbers. I'm still smiling. "Thank you. And please, call me Debra. It's great to see you, Billy."

Billy returns my smile as he steps away. "You too. Take care."

I watch after him another moment. There's a slight

stirring in my chest, a happy squeeze. A remembrance of why I began teaching in the first place.

Moments like this are a reminder that as a teacher, you get to help shape a child's life, hopefully helping them grow into the best adult they can be.

What a wonderful privilege that is. Somewhere along the way, it feels like I've forgotten about that.

I finish up the remainder of my grocery run with a lightness in my body from the interaction, almost floating down the aisles.

The feeling tapers off as I push the grocery cart through the exit doors and spot the sky overhead.

Gone are the patches of blue from earlier, replaced with more sheets of gray. It's entirely overcast now, with even darker clouds hanging low in the distance.

I try not to let the change in weather bother me too much, but it does put a bit of a damper on the day.

It would've been wonderful to have some sun, especially after last night. While we're now aware of the noises the house makes, that doesn't mean I'm looking forward to hearing all of them.

I wheel the cart toward the car with a sigh, having to wrench the rickety thing to the side a couple times to counteract one of the broken wheels.

As I load the groceries into the car, I find myself glancing back up at the sky once more.

The view overhead leaves me with a slightly uneasy feeling in my stomach.

Something is definitely coming.

NINE

Larry chews the inside of his lip as he stands in front of the pantry door, hands on his hips.

"Probably takes a few hours," he says. "Or maybe the right wind conditions."

We're both standing in front of the door that spontaneously shut last night, waiting to see if it'll shut again on its own.

For now, it remains open, and doesn't seem all that eager to repeat the creepshow.

Larry steps closer and squints up at the top corner. "It's the door jamb. It's got to be out of plumb one direction or the other. It'll close eventually. You'll see."

I nod. We've unloaded all the groceries and put them in the fridge and pantry. The extra batteries and flashlights are sitting on the kitchen counter, ready for action should we lose power.

A knock at the front door brings both our heads up. I look at Larry, and he looks at me.

"Who's that?" he asks.

I shake my head and together we walk through the house until we're in the entryway. I catch the sight of blonde hair through one of the windows as we approach the door.

Larry cracks it open, revealing an attractive woman in her late twenties, maybe early thirties.

"Where's—" The young woman's voice cuts off as she turns her head to face us again, after having looked back at our car.

She appears just as surprised to see us as we are to see her. Her mouth opens and then closes.

"Yes? Can we help you?" Larry asks.

"Um... is Kevin ...here?" she asks.

"No, he's not. We're here for the week," I say to her.

The woman's brow furrows. "Oh. I'm sorry, I must have my dates mixed up. Kevin said to meet him here today, I thought."

"Who are you?" Larry asks.

The woman gives us a smile, flashing nice straight teeth. "Sarah. I'm the cleaning lady."

"Gotcha. Well, no Kevin here right now. And I think we're all set on the cleaning for now. Thanks though," Larry says as he starts to close the door.

Sarah looks like she wants to say something else but doesn't push it, and the door closes between us. A second later, I hear her footsteps as she heads away from the door.

"I think I'm starting to understand why Kevin and his wife might've separated," Larry says, to which I slap his arm.

Peering through the windows, I don't see Sarah

anymore. I should probably send Kevin a message and let him know that she dropped by.

I step back into the living room and then peer out the back windows to the ocean beyond, watching the waves swell and crest.

The sky is still a dark gray, but there doesn't appear to be any rain.

"Why don't we go down to the beach?" I ask.

Larry looks over at me. "Right now?"

"We're here, aren't we? Might as well make the most of it."

He looks out the windows and then nods. "Alright. Hopefully the rain stays away."

It takes me a few minutes to fill the cooler with drinks and snacks, but then we're out the door. Since we're so close to the water, it will only take a few minutes to walk down the beach, Larry carrying the cooler and chairs while I carry the beach towels.

Despite the scary-looking sky, I'm encouraged. He didn't immediately shoot down the idea, which I'm taking as a good sign.

It'll be just the two of us out there, with no distractions. Given the weather, we might even have the whole place to ourselves.

What's more romantic than that?

We reach the sand, which isn't scalding on my feet for a nice change. There's one benefit to a cloudy beach day—the sand doesn't hold nearly as much heat without the bright sun overhead.

It certainly makes trekking across it a whole lot easier as we make our way down close to the water.

"Here good?" Larry asks, dropping the chairs at his feet.

We're maybe five feet from the ocean, the waves lapping the shoreline in front of us. It sounds so soothing.

A look in both directions reveals not a single other person on the beach with us.

"Our own private beach," I say, a smile on my face.

I threw a button-up on over my swimsuit, and even though there's really no sun, I take it off. It's definitely warm and humid enough. The air is practically soupy, which is probably why there's the threat of a hurricane.

I'm hoping Larry makes a comment about me in my swimsuit, but he's not even looking. Instead, he's buried in the cooler as he digs around for a beer.

Letting out a sigh, I plop down into my beach chair beside him. A breeze blows my hair directly into my face, but I'm determined to enjoy this beach day.

Larry finally fishes out his beer from the cooler and sits back with a sigh. The can hisses as he cracks the seal.

In front of us, waves crash with emphasis as they climb up the beach. I can feel a fine mist of ocean spray on my legs as we watch the hypnotic moving water.

Still no one else around, and maybe there won't be for the rest of the day.

I fill Larry in on my chance encounter with Billy Ross at the grocery store and what he had to say.

My husband nods and smiles at the right places, but it's almost like there's some sort of invisible wall between us.

He isn't truly engaging with me or what I'm saying. Listening, but not contributing in the slightest.

"Twenty years, wow," he says, taking another sip of his beer.

"Yeah," I reply, sitting back in my seat.

We fall into silence again. I move my toes through the sand, parting it like the waves. Larry seems entirely content with just sitting and drinking, so I decide to settle in for the same.

It's nice to just be in each other's company, and he did make an effort to come out here with me at least. I've got to remember that.

"Would you pass me a beer?" I ask.

Larry looks over at me and grins, then pops the cooler back open with a smile.

"Sure thing, hon."

No sooner do I have the can of beer in hand than I feel a cool raindrop strike my knuckle.

No... please.

I glance up at the sky, where the gray clouds hang heavily overhead.

"Oh—I felt something," Larry says as he looks up.

"Starting to rain. Knew it couldn't last, not with the sky looking like that."

He takes another sip from his beer with this half-smile on his face as if he's won something, and I feel a part of me contract.

"Feels like we're trying too hard to have a vacation, don't you think?" Larry adds.

I set down my beer, feeling my throat tighten.

"At least I'm *trying*, Larry. That's more than I can say of you for the last five years. If you don't even want to try, maybe I won't either."

The words come out stronger than I meant them too, but now that they're out there, I feel better.

My cards have just been laid out on the table, and it's been a long time coming.

I'm tired of pretending I'm totally fine with the state of our marriage. Tired of Larry seeming like he wants to tear down every idea I come up with.

If he's going to sit and drink and barely pay attention to me anyway, there's no reason for me to spend much more time around him.

With a huff, I push up out of my chair, my body buzzing with my declaration as I avoid looking at Larry.

I don't really feel like the beach anymore.

He doesn't say a word, remaining there with his beer in hand as I stalk back up the beach toward the path to the house.

With each step, I feel the fire that had burned so brightly within me a few minutes ago diminish a little. It's replaced with a coil of worry in my belly at what I've just done.

But no, I made the right decision telling him about my feelings, and I'm sticking to it. I'm not going to be the quiet, good girl any longer, who goes along to get along.

The sand squeaks beneath my feet as I go, and as I reach the top of the beach, I realize I left my sandals behind, under my chair.

There's no way I'm going back there though, so I just tough it out as the sand turns to dirt.

A few more drops sprinkle down, the cool touch of water tapping my forehead and arms as I walk.

The house comes into view, its gorgeous design doing

little to lift my mood. My marriage might very well be crashing down, like the waves eating away at the shoreline.

I step up onto the back porch, the weathered wooden planks rough against the soft soles of my feet. Gingerly, I get the back door open and step inside.

The house is quiet, peaceful.

So quiet that I realize I'm breathing heavily, and I don't think it's just because of the brisk walk back from the beach.

In the kitchen, I go to the fridge and open it. There are a few chilled water bottles inside, and I grab one and twist off the cap. The liquid feels glorious as it rushes down my throat, the sharp coldness of it helping to snap me out of my funk.

As I turn around though, I stop drinking mid-glug.

The kitchen closet door has closed. I stare at it, my heart thudding once against my ribs.

It was open when we left for the beach, right? Unless Larry got fed up and closed it after we waited around for it to shut on its own.

I rack my brain, but I don't remember him doing that. Now, it's definitely closed. Taking a step over to it, I wrap my hand around the doorknob and twist before pulling it open.

There's a low creak as the wooden door swings open, revealing the contents of the pantry. I take my hand off the knob and step back, but the door doesn't move.

After a few seconds of silence, I shake my head.

What am I doing? Standing here waiting for a door to close.

With everything else going on, this is absolutely the least of my concerns.

My marriage is—

I freeze, water bottle half-raised to my mouth.

A shadow just moved past a window in the dining room.

TEN

My pulse skyrockets.

"Larry? Was that you?" I shout.

My voice trembles. Two seconds pass with nothing but the sound of the wind. There's no response, but I know I saw someone.

This isn't just some phantom door or weird house-noise. *I saw something.*

Whoever is outside just crossed in front of the window, disturbing the flow of light into the room as they went. My throat is so dry as I think about it I can hardly get my mouth open to speak again.

"Lar?"

Still nothing. No one's rung the doorbell or knocked. I haven't seen any more shadows or heard anything, which means whoever's out there is just standing there up against the house.

Waiting.

I can't breathe. My thoughts are wild with panic as I swivel my head, casting my gaze around the kitchen.

Knife block. Scrambling over to it, I pull out the biggest blade of the bunch and clutch it tightly between both hands.

Where's my phone? I want to call the police.

More panic lances my heart. It's back at the beach with Larry, in the pocket of my beach chair.

Still no sound. What are they waiting for?

They know I've heard them, thanks to my shouts. I take a tiny step forward, moving enough so that I can see clearly through the windows in the dining room.

There are plenty of them, so I should be able to spot...

I lower the knife. I've found the culprit, and now a smile grows on my face as I shake my head.

Huddled in the flower box beneath the furthest window is a tiny kitten, its little body pressed up against the bug screen. I've loved cats since I was a little girl. My Dad was allergic, so I never had one growing up, but that didn't mean I couldn't still be obsessed with them.

"Hi sweet baby," I say, my voice shifting into pet-talk almost instinctually.

The kitten's head twists around so that it's looking at me, its large green eyes full of fear. Instantly I set the knife down on top of the counter beside me.

"It's okay, Mommy's gonna help," I say, taking a few careful steps closer.

Surprisingly, the kitten doesn't jump from the box and run off. As I get closer, I realize just how wet and dirty it is. My heart breaks.

The little baby must've gotten caught in the rain last night. I remember Larry telling me about a news story he saw about the feral cat population of Long Island.

This little one must've gotten separated from his family.

"It's okay," I say, keeping my voice as soothing as possible.

The kitten remains where it is, even as raindrops continue to sprinkle down. He's trying to protect himself from the rain, I think, but the wind is making it hard.

I'm at the window now, and the kitten still hasn't moved. He's just staring up at me through the screen, though as I bend down so we're just a few inches apart, he lets out a mewl.

As gently as I can, I grab hold of the bottom of the bug screen and pull it upwards. The kitten jerks back but still doesn't leave the windowbox.

I can reach him now and do so, gathering the damp baby up into my hands as I bring him inside.

There's a nice fuzzy blanket draped over the back of the couch, so I put him down on that. As soon as I do, he shakes off the droplets of rain. I watch him, biting my lip.

The poor guy.

"Is that better, baby? You came to the right place..." I trail off, trying to decide on a name.

Another gust of wind brings a sprinkling of rain drops against the window. That's it—Sprinkle. I smile.

"You came to the right house, Sprinkle," I say.

The kitten glances back at me before his pink tongue slides out of his mouth and begins licking a paw. He can't weigh more than three pounds, he's so small. I'd guess he's maybe about a month old or so.

My chest warms. Even though other parts of this

week might've been a bust, at least one good thing has come from it.

The screen door to the porch slams shut, making me shriek as I whirl around—only to see Larry standing there in the doorway, wide-eyed.

"Sorry," he says breathlessly, lowering the beach chairs down to the wooden floor.

I recover quickly from the fright, my arms crossing in front of me as I look at him. I feel, at once, embarrassed of my outburst and irritated. Larry sets down the cooler and then comes closer. Reaching the kitchen, he clears his throat.

"Listen, Deb...what you said out there... I... want to try. Okay? I want to try."

He means it, too. I can tell. Tears well at the corner of my eyes as we come together and hug.

An actual hug, one that fills my chest with warmth and hope.

"Thank you," I whisper, a tear falling down from my eye as we remain locked together.

Sprinkle lets out another meow from the couch, prompting Larry to straighten up and turn, looking for the source of the unexpected noise.

"What was that?"

I chuckle and point to the blanket and the tiny kitten sitting on top of it.

"That's Sprinkle. He was huddled in one of the windowboxes, trying to get out of the rain."

"Oh. Hi Sprinkle," Larry says, walking a few paces into the living room.

As he gets near to Sprinkle, the kitten gives a sharp

hiss, stopping him in his tracks. I watch the hackles rise across the little baby's back as he eyes Larry.

"Don't worry sweetheart, he won't hurt you. Nobody will," I say, stepping over to him.

Sprinkle calms down as I stroke a soothing hand over his coat.

Larry shrugs. "Looks like he doesn't like me."

"He just needs a little time," I assure him. "Don't you, baby?"

I scoop up the tiny cat and start toward the kitchen to see what we have on hand that he might be able to eat. Three steps from the kitchen, the lights flicker.

Larry and I look at each other, the silence stretching as we wait to see if the power flickers again. One second passes. Two. Sprinkle mewls in my arms.

Larry lets out a breath. "I think we're good."

I nod, my vision trailing over to the stack of candles piled on the console table in the hallway beside me. Larry bought them in addition to the flashlights and batteries.

Hopefully the power stays on, and we won't even need them.

Just in case though...

"Did you get matches, too?" I call over my shoulder.

"Huh?"

"Matches, for the candles."

I hear Larry murmur quietly, and then he rounds the corner and speaks again. "No, I didn't. I'm sorry. Maybe they've got some here?"

I set Sprinkle down and pull open the table's narrow drawer. Inside is a mess of wires, spare batteries, sheets of paper... and a framed college degree lying atop the rest of the pile. As if it were just swept into the drawer in a hurry.

Picking it up, I see the degree certificate is made out to Kevin Peterson. As my eyes run over it, I can't help but gasp.

"What's that?" Larry asks.

"College degree," I reply.

"But why'd you make that noise?" he asks.

I turn around and show it to him. "Because he went to Pathmore College, same as you. What are the odds of that?"

Larry shrugs. "Huh. Yeah, that's funny."

"Funny? I've never met anyone else in my *life* who's even heard of that college, let alone gone there. Isn't it weird that our host went there too?" I ask, incredulous.

"Yeah, I guess that is a weird coincidence," Larry replies. "Maybe I know him. Peterson, you said?"

"Kevin Peterson."

After another second, Larry shakes his head. "Don't remember anyone by that name."

I look down at the frame, and then at the place where it was stuffed into the drawer.

"Did you put this in here?"

Larry's eyebrows furrow. "What? Why would I do that?"

I shake my head as I put the diploma back inside the drawer and push it shut. "I don't know. Just wondering."

Larry moves past me into the kitchen. Bending and picking up Sprinkle again, I follow after my husband.

We end up giving the kitten a piece of the fish I bought at the store for dinner. He seems to enjoy it well enough, and it makes me happy to see him eating heartily.

After dinner is prepared and consumed by the human inhabitants of the house, I settle onto the couch with Larry's laptop propped on my legs again.

Darkness is beginning to fall. Beside me, Larry has the television remote in one hand and is watching the latest developments on the weather.

Luckily, things seem to be holding steady for now, which makes me feel like maybe we can still salvage at least part of this week.

Especially after our hug earlier.

There was real emotion there, I could feel it. Larry owned up, and that means a lot.

The weatherman strides across the screen in his suit pants and dress shirt, the sleeves of it rolled up and his tie removed, as they sometimes do when there's a threat of severe weather.

My guess is that he's been doing live cut-ins all day. Either that or he's trying to demonstrate how hard he's working for all of us out in living room land, like weather forecasting has caused him to work up a sweat.

Right now, he's waving vigorously at the images on the green screen behind him as he describes the projected path of the storm.

"... will make landfall later than expected," he says.

Opening up the house swap website, I navigate to the message section. As I do, Larry reaches over and gives my foot a friendly squeeze.

I look up at him and smile. He smiles back then looks

toward the TV again. It's a small, simple gesture, but it means a lot to me.

I type out a message to Kevin about discovering he went to the same college as my husband, and what a funny coincidence it is.

"Need anything?" Larry asks as he stands up from the couch.

My head shakes.

"All good," I say with a smile.

He nods and ambles off into the kitchen. When I look back down at the computer screen, I see the text bubble appear. Kevin's typing his response.

When it finally loads, my smile vanishes.

Of course I remember Larry! We were good buddies Freshman and Sophomore year. What a small world.

ELEVEN

I stare up at the ceiling as Larry snores along beside me.

Even though we already talked it over, I still can't get over Kevin's message.

Or Larry's initial insistence that he didn't remember Kevin or even recognize his name.

After I showed the message to him, he said he *might* have remembered him.

It was nearly forty years ago, sweetheart.

That is quite a substantial amount of time, I suppose. Plenty enough to forget about a person, especially one you haven't kept in contact with.

Then again, Kevin said they were *good buddies.* Not just mere acquaintances.

I'm fairly certain I could recall every real friend I've had since kindergarten if I had to.

Larry snores a little louder beside me, his lips smacking together a moment before he turns and breathes out heavily.

My gaze remains pinned on the ceiling overhead. I'm not sure what it is exactly that has me so stuck.

Maybe it's just how casual Larry was about the whole thing. Like it was no big deal he'd completely forgotten about a good friend of his.

Or that we're now spending the week in that former good friend's home.

Neither of those facts seemed to faze him all that much. In fact, I know they didn't, judging by the loudness of the snoring from beside me.

To me, though, I can't help but think about it. The strange coincidence of it all.

Thump, Thump, Thump.

My eyes snap open. I guess I must've started to drift off there for a second. My heart beats steadily in my chest as the noises echo through my mind.

This time, Larry didn't so much as stir.

I let out a breath and turn over to face the wall. If I don't want to be utterly exhausted tomorrow, I've just got to get used to the weird sounds this place makes at times.

My eyes drift down to Sprinkle, who's curled up on a blanket on the floor beside the bed. The little kitten seems sound asleep, leaving me the only one still awake at this hour.

With a sigh, I let my eyes close again. There's another round of thumping, but I will myself to ignore it, managing to keep my eyes shut this time around.

There we go—a good start.

It takes a while, but eventually I start to drift again, images of basement doors looming in my head.

———

THE NEXT MORNING, I wake up to the sun shining brightly through the window.

It's not a dream—the sky is actually looking much clearer. Turning my head to the left, I see only rumpled sheets.

Looks like Larry got an early start on the day.

I hear the faucet turn on in the adjoining bathroom, followed by a loud hum as Larry uses his electric razor. I roll over, but don't immediately see Sprinkle.

He's not on his blanket—not by the food plate or water bowl I put out for him in the room, either.

My heart beats a little faster, waking me up fully in moments.

I don't want such a little kitten exploring places on his own right now. Images of long drops and exposed electrical cords spring to mind, prompting me to push off the covers and swing my legs so my feet are on the floor.

The bathroom door opens with a creak, drawing my attention to Larry as he steps back into the bedroom.

"Was Sprinkle in there with you?"

"What? In the bathroom? No... I don't think so. He's not on the blanket?" Larry asks.

I shake my head and rise from the bed. My throat feels tight as I cast a worried glance around the room.

Where is he?

"He's just so tiny," I say, wringing my hands as I look behind the armchair beside me, "I don't want him getting into something he shouldn't."

I'm not sure why I'm so worked up. Maybe it's got

something to do with the fact I can't have kids. I guess those motherly instincts still need to express themselves somehow.

Larry looks to his right. "Check under the bed maybe?"

I dive down to my knees and pull back the bedskirt that covers the bed frame.

A furry little face stares back at me, pausing in the middle of chewing on the shoelaces of a pair of hiking boots.

Sprinkle mewls, and I breathe out heavily.

"Found him," I say, reaching under the bed to scoop him out.

My nose wrinkles as the distinct smell of excrement hits me.

"And his potty," I add.

Larry chuckles as he pulls on a shirt.

I drag out the shoes too, feeling a pang when I see the damage. Given how small Sprinkle is, I should've expected that he'd be teething.

Guilt wracks my chest as I examine the teeth marks in the heel and laces. Kevin opened his home to us, and we repaid him by ruining a pair of shoes and defecating on the floor.

Well, not us personally, but I'm responsible since I'm the one who decided to bring Sprinkle inside.

I get the mess cleaned up with some spray and paper towels. Guess I really shouldn't be surprised it happened. Starting today, I'm going to try training him to potty only on paper towels to avoid this happening again.

As far as the boots go, the damage isn't too bad. I rub

my thumb over the tooth marks, which helps a little. Still, I'll leave a note for Kevin explaining what happened and offer to pay for a replacement pair of boots.

With that settled, I glance back down at the cute culprit. Impossible to stay mad at such a sweet little face.

"Good morning baby," I say, scooping up the kitten into my arms.

Sprinkle meows his greetings back to me. As I walk to the windows, I'm amazed at how good the sky looks right now. There are visible chunks of blue between the clouds, allowing actual sunlight to stream through.

"Might actually be able to get a sunburn today," Larry says.

He's sitting on the edge of the bed behind me, putting on his socks.

"You can still burn even when it's cloudy," I say almost reflexively.

Decades of teaching fourth graders who live for recess has burned that into my brain. Nothing worse than sending a child home bright red.

After both of us are dressed, we head downstairs.

I'm feeling lighter than I have in a while, thanks to a combination of the optimistic change in weather and Larry and I finally being honest with each other yesterday.

Maybe that's the way back to each other. Honesty.

Just being open about what's wrong and trusting the other person enough to believe they won't be mad about mentioning it.

I head for the fridge as Larry grabs the TV remote off the couch and turns on the weather.

"—sunshine while you can, as unfortunately more rain is expected later today."

Aww. Looks like we aren't out of the woods just yet then. Sounds like we'll really only have a few decent hours before the cloud cover sets in again. I pull out a carton of eggs and place it on the countertop.

We'll have to hurry through breakfast and shopping for Sprinkle if we want to capitalize on the sun. Still have to get him some proper cat food, after all, and a litter box wouldn't be a bad idea.

I hear Larry padding into the kitchen behind me while I pull some eggs out of the carton.

"Listen... why don't I just run to the store?" he asks. "That way you can make the most of the weather, while it holds up."

I turn around. "Really?"

Larry nods. "Absolutely. I know how much you wanted to get out there and enjoy the beach, so enjoy it. Just tell me what to grab, and I'll take care of it."

I smile, my heart warming. Larry and I hug again as I express my thanks. The fact that he's thinking of my happiness is even better than a couple hours of sun.

"Where's your laptop? I just want to check and see what the best kind of kitten food is," I say as I stride into the living room.

The TV volume is muted now, but the weather segment is still on. Animated rain clouds obscure the day's temperature numbers as the weatherman moves across the screen.

"Should still be on the couch," Larry says from the kitchen.

I plop down and pick up one of the throw pillows, finding the laptop underneath.

With Sprinkle now in our care, I'm taking this responsibility very seriously. Whatever the best brand of food is for growing cats, that's the one we're going to get.

Probably a teething toy, too. The laptop warms my thighs as I watch the screen and wait for it to boot up.

The weatherman waves behind him, pointing at the map and wearing a dire expression. Rain, rain, rain.

At least the skies seem to be parting between Larry and me. I catch his eye as he opens the fridge, and both of us smile.

"What?" he asks.

"Nothing," I say, still grinning.

The laptop is ready to use, finally. I open a search browser and type in *best brand of food for kitten*.

There's a dizzying array of articles on the topic, so I go through a few of them, trying my best to avoid the ones that are sponsored.

After seeing the same brand mentioned several times in reviews that at least seem legitimate, I let Larry know that's the one he should look for.

"Got it," he says.

Just as I'm about to shut the computer, there's a pinging sound that draws my eyes back to the screen.

It's the email notification noise. I click over to Larry's email out of curiosity. His work never emails, so who could be reaching out?

As soon as the page loads, I really, really wish it hadn't.

TWELVE

My throat is so tight I can hardly swallow as I work my eyes over the email again.

It's from an email address made up of a random jumble of letters and numbers, but that's not what's got my chest aching.

It's the message.

Miss you, Firebird.

That's all it says, and yet those three words are enough to get my heart pounding against my ribcage.

My eyes flick up to Larry in the kitchen, his back to me as he reaches into a cupboard for a glass.

He clears his throat and cracks his neck.

I look back down at the message again.

Miss you, *Firebird.* What is that?

"Larry..." I say.

He responds without turning around. "Yeah?"

"What is this?"

My vision feels like it's wavering at the edges. Larry finally turns around and comes into the living room to join me on the couch. The laptop feels weightless in my numb hands as I extend it out to him.

Why can I hardly feel my body?

Larry reads the message but doesn't look up at me.

"What is this?" he asks.

I blink. "What do you mean, *what is this*? Did you read the message? Who is this from?"

The questions tumble out of me. I'm close to tears.

Larry opens his mouth and then closes it. His brows lower in apparent confusion. "I have no idea who it's from."

"No idea?" I ask.

He shakes his head. "None."

I'm having a hard time believing that. I'm having an even harder time getting solid breaths into my lungs. A thought strikes me then, one that shakes me to my very core.

"Is there someone else?" I ask quietly, tears running down my cheeks. "Is that why you've been distant?"

"*What?*" Larry asks in a shocked sounding tone. "Deb, you're acting insane right now. It's a random email, sent to me by mistake."

I swallow hard around the lump in my throat as I prepare to ask my next question. The one that really counts.

"Do you still love me?" I ask, my heart banging against my ribs.

"I... of course I do," Larry insists.

He says the right words, but I've known him long enough to recognize when he's not being entirely truthful with me.

There was a pause there. A hesitation.

Tiny, miniscule, but he had to think about it. That's what crushes me.

I feel like such an idiot. Here I am fighting tooth and nail to reignite the flame with my husband, not realizing he was the reason we were pulling apart in the first place.

He doesn't love me anymore, and I think I know why. There's someone else.

Someone who thinks he's a real *firebird*.

"Deb," Larry says, sliding closer to me on the couch.

I recoil instantly. My stomach curdles with nausea. I'm not sure whether to scream, cry, or throw up.

Larry's speaking again, but the words fall on deaf ears. I don't want to hear any of it.

"Listen to me," he pleads, grabbing my hand.

That pulls my attention back to him, although I can only look at him for a second before looking away.

"I've literally never heard of that email address in my life," he insists.

That doesn't exactly mean a whole lot. People cheating on their spouses probably don't go around sharing their adultery on their public email addresses.

"Look, I just blocked it," Larry says, pointing at the screen. "See? Gone."

I glance up at Larry again, finding his eyes.

There's definitely emotion there, but what's truly horrifying is, I can't tell exactly which one.

Panic? At what—losing me, or getting caught?

I thought I knew my husband. Or at least, I thought I knew that he loved me, no matter what.

Then the realization hits me. What has he done as of late to prove that fact to me?

I haven't known that as a certainty for *years* now.

Another wave of nausea rolls over me, making my stomach clench. I can't be here on this couch with him anymore. I get to my feet.

"You have to believe me," he says, standing up with me.

"Why should I, Larry? I basically had to drag you to come with me on this trip, and now I think I know why. You've got your *firebird* waiting for you back in the city."

Larry reaches out for my hand again, but I move my arm so he can't grab it. He licks his lips, trying to find my eyes.

"Deb... honey, please. I'd never do something like that. You have to believe me."

His voice breaks at the end, which I would've taken for sincerity in the past.

As much as I'd like to believe him now, I'm just not sure anymore. The only thing I am sure of is that I heard that hesitation.

That hesitation when I asked if he still loved me. I shake my head, taking a moment to steel myself.

"I'm... I'm going to the beach," I say, my words coming out shakily.

Why is it that I'm the one so affected here? Larry's the one in trouble, and here I am barely holding myself together.

He calls my name as I storm past him into the kitchen, but I don't turn around. Instead, I scoop up

Sprinkle and grab the beach bag and a chair at the door before stepping out onto the porch.

The door claps shut loudly behind me. Sunlight hits my skin, but I no longer feel free and weightless as before.

I've become the dark clouds.

More tears slip down my cheeks as I walk down the lawn toward the beach path. I don't hear the porch door open behind me, which means Larry's not following.

I don't know whether to be grateful or disappointed. I don't know anything anymore.

A thousand thoughts swirl through my head, frothing like seawater. The beach bag starts to slip, and I hike it higher on my shoulder.

Firebird. Cutesy nicknames for each other, which means inside jokes. I can hardly walk straight.

Thinking of Larry's big *heartfelt* declaration last night, I want to scream and rage and cackle like an insane person.

He must think I'm the dumbest person in the world. A complete fool.

All the time I spent worrying about him, about us. Wondering what I'd been doing wrong. Thinking maybe if I tried harder, things could go back to the way they once were.

Ridiculous. I shake my head and drop the bag and chair in a huff.

I'm a fool for ever thinking I could make this work.

The ocean looks stunning right now, but I can hardly pay it any mind as I wrench open the beach chair and plop down into it.

My brain is still smoldering with the image of that message, like its been burned into it with a branding iron.

Miss you. Miss you.

Gone three days, and she misses him. I can't remember the last time Larry told me he missed me.

Sprinkle squirms in my hands and lets out a little noise, wanting to be let down. I lower him to the sand, which is nice and cool given the lack of sun over the past few days.

I'm glad to have him here with me. Knowing I need to take care of this tiny creature is enough to pull me from my thoughts for at least a moment.

Pulling a water bottle out of the beach bag, I pour some into my cupped hand.

Sprinkle laps it up, his miniature pink tongue flicking in and out of his mouth before he falls back onto his backside, satisfied.

I let out a breath, looking down at the kitten, studying his sweet innocence.

How much I envy him. He'll never have to worry about a cheating husband, the prospect of a divorce, any of those things. I blink twice.

What am I doing?

Sagging back into the chair, I let my head rest against the back support and take another shaking breath. I have absolutely no idea what's supposed to come next, and right now, I don't think I can handle even thinking about it.

"Making the most of the sun too I see," I hear from somewhere off to my right.

My eyes come open again as I turn my head to see a woman walking toward me. It's Cheryl.

She's all smiles as she walks toward me, and I have to remind myself that everyone else's world has not just come crashing down.

For some people, the world still turns as usual and life marches on. They're simply enjoying the day, grateful for a few hours of sunshine in the midst of a stormy week.

Somehow I manage to plaster a smile on my face.

"Hello," I say politely as Cheryl walks by me, her legs blocking my view of the water for a moment.

She gives me a polite nod in return and then continues down the beach, her feet leaving clear imprints on the sand. She has her headphones in for her beach walk.

As I follow her with my eyes, I see a few more people dotting the beach in front of her. She waves to someone in the distance, and I turn away.

Human connection is not meant for me, apparently. I thought I did everything right. Stable career, marriage– and it just wasn't enough.

The tide seems to be coming in. The waves creep nearly to my chair before receding, leaving behind a white foamy layer of bubbles.

I don't know what comes next for us.

I imagine the car ride home, having to spend hours seated beside Larry in our dinky old car. Just the thought of it makes me feel nauseous all over again.

The ride home's a big enough problem in itself, let alone whatever's supposed to come next.

We get home and then what? Thirty years of marriage gone, right down the drain?

I continue to stare out at the rolling waves, various emotions rising and falling within me. The clouds move briskly across the sky overhead, though I'm hardly paying attention.

There's no lesson plan for something like this. No end of school day, either.

This is simply my life now, and somehow I've got to find a way to pick up the pieces and go on.

Time seems to lose meaning as I stare mindlessly out at the water. Minutes pass, hours maybe.

All I see, hear, and feel is the gentle spray of the water on my legs and feet. Endless ocean in front of me, churning. Tossing and turning.

A shrill ring snaps me out of my stupor, making me jump in my chair. I blink a few times to clear my head.

The sky is much darker now. Any semblance of blue is long gone.

Somehow evening has already arrived, and a fat raindrop lands on my arm to announce it.

My cell phone. That's my cellphone ringing.

Digging into my pocket, I pull out the buzzing device, wondering for a split-second if it's Larry. It's not. It's Wendy, one of our neighbors back in Queens.

"Hello?" I say, bringing the phone up to my ear.

Wendy and I are friendly, meaning we say hello when we pass by each other on the sidewalk or in the supermarket, but we don't really spend any time together.

"Hi Deb, hope I didn't catch you at a bad time," Wendy says.

"Just wanted to check and make sure you know the gate to your driveway has been sitting open for days now. I know it's a pretty safe area, but I just wanted to make sure you knew."

My brow furrows. The driveway gate? Did Kevin forget to close it?

"We're actually not at home right now," I start to explain.

"Right, that's what I figured," Wendy says. "I remember you mentioning you were leaving town for a bit. I can close it for you, if you'd like. I don't mind."

Kevin must not realize that you're supposed to close the gate doors to the driveway when you come home.

It's a pretty understandable mistake, to be honest. Most people don't live in a city like New York, and fewer still have a gate on their driveway.

"Thanks for offering, but there's no need to inconvenience yourself. I'll just let Kevin know to close it from now on," I say.

"Who's Kevin?" Wendy asks.

"Right, sorry," I say, suddenly realizing she has no idea about any of the house-swap stuff.

"Just someone staying in our place while we're gone."

Wendy is quiet for a moment. The silence stretches long enough that I glance at my phone screen to see if I accidentally hung up.

"Wendy?" I ask.

"Deb, there's no one staying at your place," she says at last. "I haven't seen a single person come or go since you and Larry left."

THIRTEEN

It takes me a moment to even process what Wendy just said.

"That's... that can't be right," I stutter, having trouble finding my words.

She must've just missed Kevin, that's all. It's not like she spends all day staring at our house.

"Deb, I'm looking out the window right now and see a pile of newspapers on the front step," Wendy says.

My heart pounds. That doesn't make any sense.

Obviously if Kevin were there, he would be picking up the newspapers each day instead of leaving them blocking the door.

"I don't..." I say, trailing off completely.

What is going on? My mind races as I try to parse through what Wendy is telling me.

Then the obvious question hits me.

If Kevin isn't at our place, then where is he?

"Deb? Are you still there? Can you hear me?"

Wendy's voice sounds far away now, barely audible above the buzzing in my ears.

"I've—I've got to go," I say, lowering the phone from my face.

"Wait! Should I close the—"

The rest of her sentence is cut off as I hang up the phone, my entire head buzzing now.

What is going on?

I don't understand. Kevin has been messaging me, telling me how wonderful our place is. How it's exactly what he was looking for.

And yet now Wendy tells me he's not there, that no one is.

No one's been there since we left.

I push out of the beach chair and get to my feet, feeling a little light-headed.

Confused thoughts stumble through my mind as I pick everything up and make my way back toward the house. As I walk, the world around me is losing light rapidly.

I need to message Kevin and figure out what's going on. There has to be some plausible explanation for all of this. Right?

Yanking open the screen door, I let it clap shut on my rear as I call out for Larry. Despite everything that's transpired between us, I still feel like I need to tell him about the startling information I just received.

There's no response. I take a few more steps into the house, calling out his name again. Still nothing.

A peek through the front windows at the driveway reveals an empty space where the car was.

Larry's gone. Maybe to the store, I don't know.

Maybe back to the city—to *her*.

Collapsing on the couch, I put Sprinkle down next to me. The little kitten watches me, meowing again.

Larry's laptop is still here, there on the cushion beside me. I eye it for a long moment, chewing my lip.

The traumatic email flashes through my mind again, making me flinch inwardly.

Still, I have to know what's going on. I reach over and scoop up the laptop and then drop it onto my knees.

It whirs as it starts up, leaving me sitting there tapping my foot. The TV is still on, still muted.

Two news anchors sit at a desk mouthing to each other. I watch them chattering for a moment before dropping my eyes back down to the screen.

Come on, wake up.

Almost like someone has turned on a faucet, the rain starts up suddenly, the wind blowing it against the windows.

It starts slow but is picking up strength with each passing second. I watch the drops hit the glass for a second before refocusing on the laptop.

Finally the computer is ready for use, and I navigate to SwapNStay.com. Then I open up messages.

Kevin, I just heard from a neighbor that the driveway gate is open and newspapers are piling up on the step. What's going on? I type out.

As usual, it notifies me that the message was read. I expect to see the text bubble pop up, but it doesn't.

The seconds stretch on, and still no response. I sit

back on the couch, blowing out a breath, trying to stay calm.

He's viewed the message but hasn't responded. What does that mean?

I lean forward to type again, my pulse pounding hard enough to make my fingers shake a little on the keys.

Kevin?

This message is instantly viewed as well. As before, there's no response.

What I should be seeing is a clear, simple explanation as to why he hasn't been seen at our place. Why he hasn't picked up the newspapers he would have to pick up in order to open the front door.

Instead, all I get is a disconcerting notification that he's viewed my message.

A cold sensation settles in the pit of my stomach.

If Kevin isn't at our home...

Where is he? Why would he lie about being there?

A peal of rolling thunder booms across the sky, feeling almost as if it shakes the very house itself.

Then another thought strikes me.

A thought more terrifying than anything I've ever imagined in my life.

What if he never left here at all?

FOURTEEN

I stiffen on the couch as my head snaps up to scan the house around me.

This unfamiliar home. Kevin's home.

My chest tightens so much I can hardly breathe, much less think straight.

It feels like there's a clamp pressing down on me as the house creaks and I clutch tightly to the couch cushion beneath me.

What if—for whatever reason—Kevin stayed here?

Fooled us into thinking he'd left.

A million thoughts rush to mind. The one rule not to go into the basement. The weird sounds in the night. I swallow hard, feeling like a powerful hand has closed around my throat.

All of a sudden, it's like the walls themselves feel alive. Watching me, inching closer. Creaking and moaning as they bear down upon me.

I look down the hallway to my right, where the staircase is. The basement door is right there. Steps away.

Unlocked.

Thunder booms again, this time accompanied by a flash of lightning that casts the house in sudden, stark illumination. The storm must be right over us.

My eyes flick to the TV, catching the news banner scrolling along the bottom.

SUDDEN FLASH FLOODING SHUTS DOWN HIGHWAYS

And then there's a *pop*, and it's darkness around me. My shriek makes Sprinkle nearly jump out of his skin.

The power's out.

My head whips to the window, where I can just make out the trees swaying in the wind through the bleary glass. The storm must've knocked down some electrical wires nearby.

I stare at the blank black TV screen, and I'm met with a faint reflection of myself.

Alone. In a dark house I don't know well.

The house creaks again, loudly. It goes on for more than a second before falling into complete silence again. I hated those sounds when the lights were on and Larry was here beside me.

Now, after what I've just learned from Wendy, it's utterly terrifying.

I sink deeper into the cushions, hoping maybe I'll be able to melt right through them and end up okay.

Somewhere else, somewhere safe.

A flash of light from outside paints the windows in a yellow glow. Not lightning. Car headlights.

Larry.

I shoot to my feet, pulse pounding as I get my bearings and then race for the front door.

The car stops in the driveway as I wrench open the front door, feeling raindrops hit me instantly. It's raining so hard, it's practically coming down sideways.

"Larry," I scream, stepping off the porch and hurrying down the path to the driveway. Puddles already an inch deep splash up my legs, but I don't care.

We just need to leave.

Larry opens the car door, the hand he holds above his head doing nothing to stop him from getting drenched.

"They closed the roads, couldn't get to the... what's going on?" he shouts to me as I stumble and nearly face-plant in my haste.

Recovering, I run toward him, stopping in front of him. My chest heaves up and down as I suck in a breath. Water pours off my brow in waterfalls.

"Kevin never showed up at our house," I say, panting.

Larry stares at me. "What?"

I nod rapidly. "Wendy just called. He never showed up."

"Never showed up? That can't be right," he says.

I shake my head. "Wendy said there's a pile of newspapers by the front door."

Larry tongues one of his molars as he thinks it all over.

"But then where..." he starts but trails off.

He's wondering the same thing I am. Kevin's got to be somewhere. If he isn't at our place, then...

Larry's eyes widen as more thunder booms.

It's so loud, I'm pretty sure the storm is boiling directly over our heads now.

My husband turns to look toward the cottage as he reaches the same conclusion I did—that Kevin might still be inside.

"You don't think..." he starts but doesn't finish.

He doesn't have to. I know what he means.

The *basement*.

My fingers twist together as we stand there in the rain. I'm soaked to the bone, but I have no intention of going back inside that house unless Larry comes with me.

"They've closed the roads," he says. "We're going nowhere, at least not tonight."

He chews his lip, eyes flicking over to the house again as more rain pours down.

Another flash of lightning. Larry hustles around to the trunk and gets it open, reappearing with a lug wrench, the cross-shaped tool gripped tightly between his fingers.

"What are you *doing*?" I ask with a gasp.

"Time to get some answers around here," he says, marching back toward the house.

"I've had quite enough of all this. We're searching every inch of this haunted house—and then we're going into that basement."

FIFTEEN

The front door creaks when it opens, as it did the first day we arrived.

Now though, there's no feeling of elation or excitement over the beauty of the place. Both of us stand in the doorway, our backs being pelted by rain. Neither of us moves.

The house is quiet, dark. Seconds pass, and then Larry adjusts his grip on the lug wrench and steps inside.

"Hello?" he shouts out to no response.

Without power, the cottage somehow seems colder, emptier. There are more shadows, more places for someone to hide.

I go in after Larry, taking a baby step over the threshold so that I'm just inside.

The door behind me stays open, letting in the din of crashing thunder and droning rain. Larry makes his way through the living room, tip-toeing forward with the lug wrench held high.

The veins in his arms pulse as he gives the metal tool

a squeeze upon rounding the corner to the kitchen. The house remains as still and silent as ever.

There's no sign of Sprinkle on the couch, which sends my pulse even higher.

As Larry creeps through the rest of the first floor and then upstairs, I drop down to my knees and start looking for the little kitten.

"Sprinkle," I hiss.

I'm hoping to hear a mew, but I don't. Thunder booms, and this time it really does shake the house. I jump, but I'm so tightly wound right now I'd jump at anything.

My eyes move to the couch, and the few inches of space underneath it.

Lowering myself down, I get my cheek as close to the floorboards as I dare and then peer underneath.

There he is—a tiny shivering ball.

The poor baby is terrified of all the noise.

"Come here sweetheart," I say hurriedly, sweeping an arm underneath to pry him out.

Sprinkle mews protests the whole way out until I tuck him against my chest.

Larry's footsteps descending the stairs behind me tell me there's no sign on anyone upstairs.

"Nothing," he says when we meet in the foyer.

"Only one place we haven't checked."

Larry licks his lips as he glances to our right. There's the basement door, which we know is unlocked, but which has remained shut the entire time we've been here.

Before I even realize what's happening, Larry's walking toward it.

"Are you sure about this?" I ask in a whisper.

He looks back at me, droplets of water still dripping off his hair.

"I need to know what's down there, if it's Kevin, or something else. But I just need to know. I won't stay another second in this house without knowing," he says.

His shoulders rise and fall. After smearing a hand across his face, Larry regrips the wrench and then turns back around.

"We're going downstairs," he says.

Before I can add anything or disagree, he takes another two steps toward the door—and collides with the corner of the hall table, knocking over the vase on top of it.

It crashes to the hardwood floor in a shattering of porcelain. My body tenses as Larry looks back at me, eyes wide.

If Kevin *is* downstairs, he's certainly going to know we're coming.

Rubbing his hip, Larry recovers his posture and then steps over to the door and grabs the doorknob.

I expect him to yank it open, but he doesn't.

A second passes, and then two. Larry's hand remains on the knob. He's just standing there.

Thunder claps behind me, followed by a flash of lightning that illuminates the entryway around me for a moment.

Larry looks back at me, panting lightly as our eyes meet in the dark interior.

It's still completely silent, save for the crashing thunderstorm outside. In here, it's akin to a graveyard. Mud is scattered throughout the entryway from our shoes.

With another short exhale, Larry regrips the doorknob and twists it. The door opens easily, providing no resistance whatsoever. There's a little creak as it swings wide.

My entire body tenses as Larry stands there, ready to face the full brunt of whatever is behind the door... but nothing happens.

I watch as his shoulders lower. He was expecting something, too. Or someone.

But it's just as silent as before. After another second, I take a few cautious steps forward, Sprinkle still cupped protectively against my chest.

Larry peers into the dark opening but doesn't move his feet.

"Can you see anything?" I whisper.

He shakes his head.

Another couple steps, and then I'm standing beside him.

Our eyes meet, and then both of us turn to look down into the black abyss before us.

SIXTEEN

Larry reaches into his pocket and pulls out a flashlight.

He offers it to me, and I take it. Flicking my thumb over the power button throws a narrow circle of light onto the wall.

I readjust my grip on Sprinkle and then move my other arm so that the beam of light is pointing into the open basement doorway.

The light reveals a blank wall across from us. Two stone steps descend to a small landing, where more wooden steps then trail down into the darkness to our right.

Larry shifts his weight between his feet and switches the lug wrench to his other hand, smearing his left palm against his pant leg.

"Let's do this," he says.

He steps down onto the first step and immediately wrinkles his nose.

"Smells damp," he says.

Just as he says it, the smell reaches me too. It's a wet, earthy smell. Mold probably.

Larry takes another step down onto the landing, and I'm right behind him. There's barely enough room for us both to stand there, We're pressed up against each other, our wet shirts rubbing together.

I hold up the flashlight and shine it down the rest of the steps before us.

The light reveals at least twenty steps down, as well as a few wooden support beams on the sides to hold the structure up. The light also reveals the basement floor at the bottom, which looks like it's made of cement.

"Hello?" Larry shouts, his voice high and tight.

No response but the muffled pounding of the rain on the roof overhead. Another second passes, and Larry takes another step.

It's so deathly quiet down here.

The further down we go, the more it seems like the world around us has been swallowed up entirely. The sounds of the storm fade out the lower we go, until it's just a distant memory.

The darkness is almost overwhelming. It seems to press in from all angles, practically beating back the dim flashlight beam as I keep it on a swivel.

Once we're past the tenth stair, the walls open up and we're able to get a look at the basement through the studs.

My lungs start to burn, but I'm afraid to breathe as I whisk the flashlight over the space.

There's... nothing.

Well, almost nothing. The walls and floor are

completely barren, save for a single folding table off to our right. I move the flashlight over some concrete steps that lead up to the backyard, and that's it.

It's just a bare, unfinished basement.

"What?" Larry asks in a normal tone.

It sounds oddly given how quiet we've been. He steps off the staircase onto the concrete floor and looks around.

"There's nothing here," he says, clearly confused.

I am as well. Given everything we've been through in the past few days, there were a couple of things I wouldn't have been surprised to find down here.

Kevin's wife's body, for starters. Perhaps Kevin himself. But there's nothing but the folding table.

My eyebrows draw together as I cast the light around the room again.

Kevin is most definitely not here.

If he isn't here, and he isn't in our house, where is he?

It doesn't make any sense. Why would he lie about where he was?

And why all the warnings and secrecy for... what? Some random garden tools?

I join Larry near the folding table. Spread across the surface of it are four ordinary, hand-held gardening tools.

A spade, a garden fork, a trowel, and a pair of shears.

Larry picks up the garden fork and examines the three tines before dropping it back down to the table.

"I don't get it," he says.

"Why tell us we can't come down here? I could buy these tools for fifty bucks at the hardware store."

None of it makes any sense at all. The lying, the

deception. It's like there's some piece of this that I'm just not getting.

Larry starts toward the door to the back yard, and I follow after him, centering the light ahead of us so we can see.

There are concrete steps, and then the two metal bulkhead doors that lead into the yard. Water darkens the concrete on either wall where the doors meet the sides. Leaking.

That explains why it smells so rank down here.

Larry puts a foot on the first concrete step and reaches up to try the doors. They move an inch or so before stopping. Padlocked from the outside.

After another minute of examination, Larry and I move back to the center of the room.

"Well, at least we know the house is empty," he says, shrugging.

"But where's Kevin? And why would he lie about where he is?" I press.

Larry shakes his head. "I don't know. But it stinks down here, so we should go back upstairs."

He starts across the concrete floor to the staircase again. I sweep the flashlight around once more, just in case there was anything we might have missed. I keep expecting to see someone leap out at me, but there's nothing. Just an empty, musty room.

I let out a breath and then follow Larry. As terrified as I was of venturing downstairs, I was looking forward to at least having some sort of clarity.

I'd thought maybe we'd come across the body of Kevin's wife, and everything would start making sense.

Some smoking gun that would explain the secrecy, the sneaking around.

But now, I'm left with more questions than answers. Our host took great care in explaining that we were permitted to go anywhere other than down here, which naturally made me think there was some reason.

I shake my head as we march back upstairs. I don't know. I don't get it and don't know if we ever will.

The moment it stops absolutely blustering outside and the roads open, we're leaving.

I don't care how awkward the car ride might be, I'm tired and anxious and tired of feeling anxious.

This was *not* the week I was hoping for, but I'm beyond that now.

Back on the first floor, Larry waits until I'm out and then pulls the basement door closed behind me. He looks at it for a second and then turns to me, chewing his lip.

"So, with the roads shut down, it's gonna be a while until we can go."

I nod silently and adjust the hand holding Sprinkle. Larry looks at me.

"Maybe we could—"

"I'd like to be alone," I interject.

With the pressing question of the household head-count answered, I'm once again able to think about the other stuff. The betrayal.

Our immediate safety took precedence, but now that we know Kevin isn't here, I can hardly stand to be in the same room as Larry.

All I can think about is *miss you, Firebird*. My throat

aches. He doesn't love me anymore. He's here out of duty alone.

Larry swallows and then nods, stepping silently around me before going up the stairs. I hear the bedroom door open and shut.

Once I'm sure that he's not coming back to try to talk me into something, I move out of the hallway and into the dining room. I switch on one of the electric lanterns, which casts the room in a ghastly white light that reminds me too much of a hospital.

Hurriedly I light a few candles and disperse them throughout the first floor. They throw off a much warmer glow.

The floorboards creak overhead as Larry moves around upstairs. I flick my eyes up but then force my attention to my surroundings in the kitchen. It doesn't matter what he's doing up there, whether he can sleep.

I'm done with him.

Even if he wants to make up now, it's too little, too late.

More and more, I'm remembering how little true love he's showed me over the past few years. Really, the email should've come as no surprise.

I'm almost tempted to run over to the couch and open up the computer to search for more, but why torture myself?

I *saw* the hesitation in his eyes, heard it in his voice. That told me everything I need to know.

A relationship without two invested parties isn't a relationship at all.

Even with the candles, I don't exactly feel cozy in the

house. There's a window open somewhere. I can see the breeze causing the flames to flicker and hear the sound of water pouring down outside a little too well.

With the storm getting as bad as it is, I need to find it and make sure all the windows are shut tight before we drown in here. If the weather forecasters can be believed, it's only going to get worse.

The candles throw a little light around the kitchen, but even still, it's so dark and full of shadows. They seem to seep in from the corners, trying to engulf everything in their night.

I've had just about enough of quaint old houses, I think.

Picking up the flashlight again, I start toward the noise, moving into the living room, searching for the open window so I can close it. I just need—

A spear of panic lances through my chest, freezing me in place. What was that?

The blood rushing through my ears is so loud I can hardly hear anything now, but I swear I heard a splashing sound outside.

Swallowing hard, I flick my eyes between the dark front windows, looking for the source of the noise. They reveal nothing but swaying trees and heavy rain.

Must've been my mind playing tricks. It feels like the whole world is made of water at this point.

And then just as I turn away from the windows, something *moves* in my peripheral vision.

SEVENTEEN

I drop down beside the couch with my breath frozen in my chest.

Someone just walked by a window. I know it. I *saw* it.

This isn't just some weird creaking. This is real. It was definitely a person. My mind races as I strain my hearing.

Someone's out there, and they're trying to get in.

No, not just someone—Kevin. He's back.

There—splashing footsteps. He's rounding the house. Why is he rounding the house?

My throat goes dry. The back porch, and the kitchen door that leads out to it—did we lock it?

No—no—no—think Debra think. But I can't, my brain is mush.

Only seconds until he's on the back porch.

A flash of lightning illuminates the coffee table and dark TV screen in front of me. One of the beer bottles on it reflects the living room. I grab it in a sweaty hand and leave the cover of the couch arm to half-squat, half crawl into the kitchen area.

The back porch is right in front of me, visible through the screen door. Even in the dark, I can just make out the stormy sea in the distance—and then the view is obscured as Kevin reaches the back steps.

He's here. He's back. He's *coming*.

I flatten myself against the fridge, my entire body buzzing. I'm about to hyperventilate I think, but somehow I manage to hold onto the beer bottle clutched upside-down in one hand.

Thud, thud. Quick footsteps across the deck. I hear the porch's screen door creak open.

More footsteps, muffled this time as he crosses the outdoor rug laid across the wooden floor of the porch.

Two seconds later he's at the kitchen door, just outside it.

My hand is so soaked in sweat I'm terrified the glass bottle is going to slip out of my grip altogether.

There's no time. I can't think, can't breathe.

Kevin's frame fills up the window in the door, blocking every ounce of light from outside. The knob turns, slowly. Gently.

There's a click, and my stomach practically falls out. The door's unlocked.

I squeeze the bottle tight enough that I can't feel my hand anymore. I will not go down without a fight.

Thunder booms again overhead, shaking the kitchen and rattling the utensils in their drawers as the door swings open.

I'm just inches away from him, but in the near pitch-darkness of the kitchen, I'm hidden. If he looks over this way, I might not be for much longer.

I don't wait for that to happen. The moment I hear his shoe come down on the kitchen floor, I lift my arm, swinging hard with a scream-grunt at his silhouette.

The bottle smashes into some part of him—it's too dark to tell what—shattering apart in my grip as my scream ends.

Kevin crashes hard to the floor at my feet and then doesn't move at all.

Standing there in the darkness, gasping for air, I feel something warm roll down over my clenched fist.

Did that just happen?

"Deb?"

I jump and spin around, but then I recognize the voice. Larry, from somewhere upstairs.

I pant hard, slowly unclenching my hand. Shards of glass land on the kitchen floor as I stare at Kevin's motionless form in front of me.

It's still so dark, I can hardly see him.

A panicked thought races across my mind. What if he's dead?

What if I just killed him in his own house?

I stumble backward then take staggering steps over to the candle on the other side of the kitchen. As I reach out to grab it, my palm lances with pain.

Wincing, I look down at my hand in the candlelight. It's covered in blood.

Larry's footsteps are quick and heavy on the staircase as he races down.

"What's going on?" he shouts. "Where are you?"

"Kitchen," I shout back, my voice strangled and hoarse.

The knife block is next to the candle, and I pull one out before turning back around to face Kevin. He might wake up at any moment.

As I bring the light closer to his body, the knife drops from my grip. It clatters to the floor at my feet as I come to a stop.

I am paralyzed. I can do nothing but stare.

Larry appears in the entryway between the living room in the kitchen. He looks first to me, his mouth opening to speak before he catches sight of the full scene. Of the body on the floor.

He blinks, stunned.

I'm stunned too. Because it wasn't Kevin who was trying to get inside. Not at all.

Sprawled out motionless on the kitchen floor is *Sarah*.

EIGHTEEN

Larry stares at her, wide-eyed.

"That's the girl. Who came to the door," he says. "The house cleaner."

I nod silently.

"Sarah," I reply, my voice barely above a whisper.

The candle's glow reveals dark blood pooled around her face. Shards of glass are all over the floor, her legs, her raincoat.

It looks like I hit her square on the back of the head.

"She tried to come in? What was she thinking?" Larry asks as he follows her muddy footsteps to the porch.

"Is she dead?" I squeak.

Larry looks back at Sarah. "I don't know."

"Check. Please... just check," I say.

Larry gives me another wide-eyed glance, and then squats beside Sarah.

She still hasn't moved an inch since I hit her. I watch

as Larry slowly extends his hand toward her neck, his fingers pressing against the skin to feel for a pulse.

"She's breathing," he says after a second. "I can feel it. Just out cold."

"What was she doing?" I ask, my voice practically begging.

My hands come up to my hair as all of it starts to sink in. Blood is everywhere and still running down from the cut in my palm.

Larry shakes his head, unable to come up with a response. I can't figure out a logical reason why the house cleaner would've been trying to sneak in through the back like that, either.

Larry licks his lips and then glances back up at me. "Is there any rope around?"

I stare at him. "For what?"

"To tie her up," he says.

"*What?*"

He gestures at Sarah. "Think about it, Deb. Everything weird that's been going on, and now she's sneaking in here? No way that's coincidence."

"But tie her up?" I ask.

My stomach is in knots, but I think about what he's saying.

Something strange is definitely going on around here. I think back to what Cheryl said, about how no one had seen Kevin's wife in a while. And then hot, sexy Sarah comes to the door asking for Kevin.

Now she's back, unannounced, during a storm in the dark of night.

My stomach clenches as I look at her again. Larry's right. Something weird is going on.

"We tie her up, keep an eye on her until the police can get here," Larry says, a little breathlessly.

"Which might be a while, given the storm outside. Where's your phone?"

I pat my pockets, but it's not there. Spinning around, I swing the candle over the length of the kitchen countertop to try and spot it, but I still can't find it.

"Give me a second. What about yours?" I ask over my shoulder as I walk back into the living room.

"Dead. Forgot to charge it last night, and then no power today means I can't charge it," he replies.

I look over the length of the couch and the coffee table, and yet still find no phone.

Sprinkle looks up at me with interest as I scurry around the room, searching every conceivable place I could've left it. And yet, nothing.

With a sigh, I raise my hand and rub my forehead as if that might produce a magical phone-finding genie.

"I can't find it. I don't know what's going on."

"Okay... listen, we'll find it. But first we need to deal with Sarah before she wakes up. Help me lift her," Larry says.

I rejoin him in the kitchen. As the candlelight reveals all the blood spred across the floor, I nearly vomit.

"There's so much blood," I say, gagging.

"Help me," Larry hisses as he starts to heave.

Stumbling over to Sarah's feet, I get my hands around her ankles and lift. She's heavier than I expect, and flops like a crash-test dummy as we prop her upright.

"Where are we gonna put her?" I ask.

Blood drips from the back of her head onto the floor. Larry licks his lips as he takes a second to think.

"Downstairs," he says.

"That way if she gets out of the rope, she can't escape through a window or something. The bulkhead doors are padlocked from the outside, so the only way out of the house is back up the stairs."

With a nod, I start backing through the entryway to the living room. Larry and I gasp and wheeze our way through the room to the main hallway and somehow manage to maneuver ourselves until we're standing right outside the basement door.

Larry darts out a bloodied hand to grasp the small doorknob, nearly losing Sarah altogether as her total weight comes down on his one hand. He balances her against his knee and darts his hand out again, this time finding a grip.

He pulls open the door and then looks back at me. I can only stare back with wide eyes, every muscle and tendon in my arms on fire as I try not to drop Sarah's legs.

Larry starts down the stairs, going backwards with his head craned to try and see.

There's hardly any light at all down here. Only a single candle in the hallway near the door provides a dim glow, and it doesn't reach all the way to the bottom.

We continue down the stairs, nearly dropping Sarah once more as our arms are ready to give out. Finally Larry reaches the bottom, though I can hardly make him out in the dim light.

"One more step," he says through gritted teeth.

I take it, and then I'm on the concrete basement floor.

"Okay, lower," he hisses, and the two of us set her down on the floor.

"Grab a chair and some rope, I'm gonna get candles," Larry rasps, doubling over with his hands on his knees.

I shoot back up the steps, my hands tingling. Chair, chair, chair.

Turning into the dining room, I grab hold of the first chair I see and pull it out from underneath the dining table. One of the legs knocks against the wall, scraping it. A few days ago, that would have freaked me out. Now, I hardly notice.

Dragging the chair into the hall, I start looking left and right.

Rope. Where would that be?

The porch. There's a bunch of nautical cord out there.

I shoot through the house as Larry comes back up the stairs behind me. Out on the porch, I pull as much cord as I can and then come back inside.

"Deb," I hear Larry call from the basement.

"Coming," I shout back.

He's already taken the chair downstairs. My legs are heavy as I step down into the basement again, feeling the temperature drop noticeably as I get below ground.

Larry has lit three candles and has a flashlight in hand as he holds Sarah upright in the chair. He waves me forward.

Handing off the rope, I take on the next challenge—figuring out how to actually get it secure around her. I was never a Girl Scout or a sailor, and I've certainly never tried to tie an unconscious person to a chair before.

Larry loops the cord around her chest, but has to take his arms off her to do so, and Sarah starts to fall forward.

He manages to catch her as I gasp.

"Help," he says.

Taking an uncertain step forward, I loop the cord around and then bring it back around to the front. Larry takes it with his free arm and does the same on the other side.

We repeat this process until we run out of rope, and Larry starts to knot the end.

"Is it gonna hold her?" I ask, chewing my lip as I take a step back, watching him.

Larry lets out a breath. "I don't know. Hopefully. I double-knotted in the back."

Sarah's chin is buried in her chest, her upper half-leaning forward against the ropes which are pulled taut with the pressure of holding her inert body.

Much of her blonde hair is matted with blood and captured dust from the cellar floor.

"What now?" I ask. "Should—"

I'm interrupted by a low groan from Sarah as she starts to regain consciousness.

NINETEEN

Larry and I watch in silence as Sarah's head slowly comes up.

"What..." she mumbles.

Her eyes open and shut once, and then two or three times in rapid succession as she comes back to the present. Her gaze takes in the cords tying her to the chair, and then she looks around, her eyes wide and terrified looking. Her raincoat crinkles as she shifts.

"What's going on?" she asks in a panicked voice.

I'm trying to get a read on Sarah, but it's tough. She seems legitimately confused, but some of that could be due to the head wound.

We need to figure out why she's here.

"I think that's what we should be asking you," Larry says, his arms crossed in front of him as he stands in front of her chair, looking down.

Sarah blinks again, wincing as she pushes against the ropes.

"What? What do you mean?"

"What do you mean, *what do I mean*? You just broke into our house," Larry says sternly.

At that, Sarah flicks her bright blue eyes up at him then over at me.

"This isn't *your* house. It's Kevin's," she says. "And I didn't break in. The back door was unlocked."

She tries the ropes again, but they don't budge. "You people are insane. Let me out of here."

"Well Kevin's not here right now," Larry says, "so for all intents and purposes, it's our home. And so what if the back door is unlocked? What are you doing sneaking into here at night in the middle of a thunderstorm?"

At that, Sarah stops struggling. She glances back up at us, her narrowed blue eyes moving between us.

"He's not here?"

Larry's brow furrows. "Who? Kevin? No, he's not. Why are *you* here?"

Now it's Sarah's turn to furrow her brow. "Because... Kevin texted and invited me to come over until this storm blows over. He told me to come through the back because you guys were trying to sleep, or something."

Larry and I exchange a glance as my heartbeat quickens. Once again, more messages from Kevin.

"Kevin texted you... saying to come *here*?" Larry asks in confirmation.

Sarah nods. "Yeah. He said the whole thing the other day was a mix-up, and he was renting out the spare bedroom to you guys to save money during the divorce."

My chest pounds as I digest her words. If she's telling the truth, Kevin is once again pretending to be somewhere he's not. First at our place, and now here.

What in the world is going on?

"Okay, so Kevin invites you over to ride out the storm with him. Why does he ask the cleaning lady?" Larry asks pointedly.

It's clear he suspects, just as I do, that there's more going on here. Sarah isn't just the cleaning lady, I'd bet money on it.

She turns her chin up. "Because he's a nice guy. The place I'm renting sucks, and I can't stand my roommates. Even less so during a power outage."

"So you aren't with Kevin," Larry says in a leading tone.

Sarah's mouth opens but then closes again. Then her shoulders slump. "Okay, fine. Yeah, we've been seeing each other, okay?"

I shake my head as Larry takes a step forward. It's the answer we both knew was true, but why didn't she just admit to it earlier?

All her shadiness about their relationship did was create more doubt in my mind about her true intentions here.

"Why did you lie just now?" Larry asks.

Sarah scoffs. "Because I don't know you? I don't just go telling my private business to anyone. Plus, you know, Kevin's still technically married until the paperwork goes through."

Larry looks back toward me, chewing his lip. A few silent words pass between us.

We can't trust her.

He rubs his forehead with two fingers and then lets out a sigh.

"I don't know what to think," he says. "So what's going to happen is this...we're all gonna wait here until the police come, and they can figure this all out."

Sarah's eyes widen instantly.

"*What?* No. You've got to untie me right now. Let me go," she hisses.

She lunges forward against the ropes with more strength than I would have expected. I jerk in surprise at the show of strength.

Sarah is not nearly as weakened as she's been leading us to believe.

"Let—me—go," she hisses between clenched teeth, wrenching her body left and right against the ropes.

Miraculously, Larry's double-knot seems to be holding. He crosses his arms again.

"Why are you so concerned about the police showing up? What have you done?" he asks.

"Let me go," Sarah says again, this time a shout.

The sharp noise echoes through the small damp basement and makes my ears ring. Larry winces too.

"Stop shouting," he says.

"Untie me right now," Sarah screams.

The sound is nearly ear-splitting. Larry tries to say something, but it's impossible to make out his words above the ruckus. After another moment of trying, he looks over to me and then jerks his chin at the stairs.

"Let me go right now," Sarah shouts after us, the words ringing through my skull as we hustle back up the stairs.

I'm trembling as I reach the first floor again. Her

whole demeanor completely changed as soon as we mentioned the police.

Larry shuts the door behind me, which cuts off the noise-level considerably, though it's still easy to make out her shouts from the floor below.

Larry blows out a long breath, his head shaking. "I don't know what's going on. Let's just find your phone so we can call the police."

Nodding silently, we move back into the living room and restart the search.

My mind is still on Sarah downstairs, whose muffled cries can still be heard over the storm. She must be in some kind of trouble with the cops.

That makes me wonder even more what her true purpose coming here was.

My throat closes as I run through a list of possible reasons she would have snuck into the house, and none of them are good.

I shake myself and look back down at the couch cushion in my hand. Sprinkle meows beside me, watching me with a tilted head as the kitten tries to figure out what I'm doing.

I jam my hand into the space between the seat cushions, hoping my fingers will brush up against the hard plastic case of my phone, but they don't.

After doing that, cushion by cushion to no avail, I get down onto my knees and peer underneath the couch where I found Sprinkle before.

No phone there, either.

Letting out a sigh, I straighten up again.

"I don't know where it could be," I say to Larry who reemerges from the kitchen, shaking his head.

This is really starting to bug me now. A phone doesn't just get up and walk away.

I might not be twenty, and therefore joined at the hip with the thing, but I'm usually pretty good at keeping it within arm's reach. I literally don't know where it could've gotten to.

With Larry's phone dead and mine missing, we can't get a call out to the police. It's looking more and more like we're just going to have to wait for the power to come back on.

After searching the entirety of the first floor, I throw up my hands in defeat. It's like the phone has disappeared into thin air.

I don't know what's going on exactly, but between the girl in the basement, Kevin's weird behavior, and now my missing phone, I've got a deep pit of worry in my stomach.

"We should keep an eye on that basement door," Larry says with a nudge of his chin.

I nod again, busying myself with relighting one of the candles that has blown out.

"Listen... Deb," Larry says from behind me.

I turn around to face him. He stands in the doorway to the kitchen, shadows flickering across his face from the candlelight.

"About earlier..." he starts.

My head shakes back and forth almost instantly. "I don't want to talk about this right now, Larry."

With everything else going on, the last thing I want

to think about right now is our broken relationship. There are so many hundreds of thoughts smashing through my brain, and I really don't think I can handle any more.

Larry chews his lip, but nods. "Okay, but I'm not going to leave you alone down here again."

I want to argue that I would rather be by myself but am immediately reminded of the chaos of the last hour. I may not want to be near him, but being alone under these circumstances would be worse.

"Fine," I relent.

Plopping onto the couch, I draw Sprinkle into my lap. Larry takes the chair and ottoman off to my right.

As I settle, I realize that Sarah has finally stopped shouting.

Besides the unrelenting rain against the window, the only other sound is the occasional boom of thunder. It no longer sounds like it's coming from directly above us, which is just about the only piece of good news I can think of.

I work hard not to look at Larry, instead focusing on Sprinkle in my lap. The little kitten gnaws at my fingers, soothing that teething pain again. I'm grateful for the distraction.

There's nothing to do now but wait.

Wait for my phone to ring, wait for the power to come on, wait for the storm to pass. Just wait. I'm not sure how much time passes with us sitting there in silence, waiting.

At one point, there's a dull crack from somewhere outside that draws our eyes. I watch as a large branch breaks off in the storm to land behind our car in the driveway.

Great. Just what we needed.

"At least it didn't hit the car. With how stingy our insurance is, I don't know if they would've covered it," Larry mutters, his eyes still focused on the debris.

I say nothing. Turning from the window, I plop back down onto the couch in exhaustion.

My eyes ache in my skull. It's been almost twenty-four hours now since I've slept, and my sleep wasn't exactly stellar before that.

Now that we have finally have a moment of relative peace, my body is crying out for rest.

Larry must read my mind, because he says, "If you want to try and sleep, I'll take the first watch."

He may not love me, but he knows me.

Part of me wants to tell him off, tell him I'm fine, but really I'm not. I'm utterly and completely drained.

"You sure?" I ask.

He nods. "I'll be fine."

He stands up and gets behind his chair to push it a few feet closer to the main entryway, trying to improve his line of sight to the basement door in this dim light.

"It's fine, Deb. Get some sleep," he assures after noticing me glancing over at him.

I don't need any more encouragement. Neither of us wears a watch, so without the microwave clock display or our phones, we have no idea what time it is. I'd have to guess close to one or two in the morning.

Despite my fatigue, there's still some part of my brain that screams at me to remain vigilant. Like at any moment, some new threat could emerge from the shadows.

Still, after a few minutes, my head bobs. Each time it does, it feels heavier and heavier.

Opening my eyes, I look up at Larry again. He's facing the basement door, keeping watch, looking deep in thought. The candles create shadows that dance across his jaw.

My eyelids weigh a hundred pounds each. Even Sprinkle lays his head down, his tiny eyes shutting in my hands as I gently stroke his fur. The motion feels almost automatic by now.

The rain in the background serves as a natural sound machine, a constant white noise that finally lulls me into a state of rest despite my mind still resisting.

Bang.

My head snaps up, the noise still ringing loud and clear through my mind.

I blink hard to clear the sleep from my eyes as I try to sit up, only to hiss as a crick in my neck sends a spike of pain down my spine.

Larry's also straightening up with a jerk. Looks like he couldn't manage to stay awake either.

The fact that he's also been jolted awake tells me that sound wasn't just in my dream.

My eyes flick down to my stomach—no Sprinkle. Where is he?

"Sprinkle?" I croak, wincing again as I sit higher on the couch.

"Larry, Sprinkle is gone again."

Larry looks over at me, looking as if he's struggling to

process my words in his newly awake state. His eyes move past me to the windows, which let in a weak light.

"What time is it?" he asks, his eyes bleary.

"I don't know. Help me look," I say, pushing off the couch.

This little kitten seems to love to spike my heartrate. It's really the last thing I need right now, but I have to find him.

"Deb," Larry says, blinking hard and then rubbing a hand across his eyes.

I look over at him. "You see him?"

He's not looking at me. He's looking into the hallway. Larry swallows hard.

"The basement door... it's open."

TWENTY

I scramble back to my feet and join him by the ottoman.

When I do, I can see what he sees, and my heartrate skyrockets.

The basement door is ajar. *Open.*

I can't do anything but stare, my vision blackening at the corners as wind pushes more rain against the house.

The hallway candle illuminates the door but does nothing to penetrate the creeping darkness that seems to seep out from the cracked opening.

The night is playing tricks on my exhausted brain and eyes. It's like tendrils of shadow are slowly oozing outward from the basement door, along with the dank smell.

"Sprinkle must've pawed it open," Larry says quietly from beside me. He hasn't moved from his chair.

"Sprinkle weighs less than five pounds, Larry," I say, my voice quivering.

Even still, there's a chance that's what's happened, right? Sprinkle *is* quite the explorer.

The door really isn't all that heavy. It could swing right open.

It's deathly silent in the house.

It occurs to me that we haven't heard a word from Sarah in what has to be hours now.

No shouting, no screaming. Nothing but the rain.

The pit in my stomach expands into the size of a fist. I look over at Larry, whose eyes are wide.

"Sarah?" Larry calls out.

I wait for her to curse us out, demand she be set free. But there's no response. Just the endless darkness of the crack in the doorway.

I'm close to hyperventilating, my entire body covered in goosebumps.

"Sarah, are you down there?" Larry shouts again.

My hands twist together. "Why isn't she responding, Larry?"

He shakes his head.

"Maybe she escaped," he whispers.

My head shakes now. "We would've heard something, right? Footsteps? And I doubt she would've just let us sleep."

I begin to spiral. What if something's happened to her?

Did we tie her too tightly? Did she somehow asphyxiate? Did the crack on her head cause a brain bleed or something?

She's not responding, which means something is wrong.

As Larry rises from his chair, I'm grabbing tight to his

shirt, my fingers squeezing the fabric so tight it's about to tear.

I stay right with him as he takes a step toward the hallway, his gaze locked on the lug wrench still leaning against the base of the staircase.

My heart is in my throat as together we creep closer to the door, ears straining for any noise from below.

It's almost impossible to distinguish any sounds with the weather outside, but I need to know why she isn't responding.

Is she even still down there?

Larry reaches out and opens the door the rest of the way. It lets out a slow creak that seems to stretch on for seconds as we stand there facing the abyss.

It's absolutely pitch-black down there.

All the candles that were lit downstairs are out. Why are they out?

Larry reaches into his pocket and pulls out a flashlight, the button-click breaking up the silence as the beam cuts into the night.

"Sarah?" he shouts down the stairs.

Not a sound from below. Just emptiness. A void.

If we want answers, we'll have to step into it.

Larry glances back at me once more and then takes the first step down. I'm still clutching onto the back of his shirt, feeling like if I let go, I'll be lost in the darkness forever.

He shines the flashlight over the steps, crouching a little to try and peer down into the basement itself. A few more steps, and then he sucks in a breath.

"The chair isn't there. She isn't there."

I stare at the empty space on the floor where Sarah had previously sat, illuminated in the dull glow of the flashlight. One of the candles has been knocked over, wax spilled out across the floor.

We descend another two steps. My entire body feels like a tight wire, every muscle tensed. I can barely move, and yet I do.

Larry slides down another step, flicking the flashlight over the length of the room in front of us.

"She's not—" he starts, but his voice cuts off.

"What?" I ask, my jaw clenching.

I follow the flashlight beam to the circle of light on the floor. Dark splotches paint the cement. My heart leaps up into my throat.

Blood. That's blood.

Larry slowly directs the flashlight up, zeroing in on another sticky patch a few inches away. He continues moving the beam to the right, following the path of blood-stains until—

He jerks, and I shriek.

But it's Sprinkle, the kitten's eyes like metallic saucers as they reflect in the glow.

Then he lowers his head to keep lapping at the blood-stain. I rush over to him and pick him up, the little cat letting out a meow of protest. His paws feel sticky in my hands.

Larry brings the flashlight around again, continuing to follow the path of the blood. The light moves nearly in a complete circle, and then we see it.

Larry's breath whooshes out beside me, and I can do nothing but stare, my knees going weak.

The flashlight beam is pointed near the steps up to the bulkhead doors at the far back of the basement.

Its glow just manages to illuminate the chair, turned on its side, facing away from us.

Sarah's body is completely motionless, her raincoat unmoving in the light.

TWENTY-ONE

The flashlight quivers in Larry's hand as he tries to hold the circle of light steady over Sarah in the chair.

"Sarah?" he asks.

She remains unmoving, facing away from us. There's more blood around the chair, and on her raincoat.

The cords that held her are now strewn about the cement floor near the chair. It's a horrible image, but I can't stop staring.

My mind races as we take a step closer, trying to figure out what could've happened. Did she try to escape, hurting herself in the process?

Larry calls her name again, but Sarah doesn't move a muscle.

The closer we get, the more blood I see. It's absolutely everywhere, darkening the cement like spilled paint. Sprinkle mews in my hands, and I hold him tight to my chest.

Larry and I take another step toward Sarah. I'm

unable to tear my eyes away. More than anything, I just want her to move.

Please, just move.

I don't care if she pops awake and screams death threats at us, as long as she's still alive. The longer I look however, the more I realize I already know her state.

I think she's dead. Dead, when we were supposed to be watching her, waiting for help to arrive. I still can't fathom how this could've happened.

All this blood. It's everywhere. Pools of it. The head wound must have been much more severe than I realized.

My knuckles are white as I clutch onto Larry's forearm. I think I'm hurting him, but he doesn't say a word as we draw even closer.

We're nearly right on top of her now, and there still hasn't been a single sign of life.

"What could've happened?" Larry whispers, voicing his thoughts aloud.

I don't have an answer. We come to a stop just in front of her.

Both of us hold our breath as he slowly eases us around her head to the other side of where she's lying so we can get a look at her face. I almost don't want to look— I've never seen a dead person before.

Are her eyes open? Closed?

How could this have happened?

When Larry shines the light down however, it's not what I'm expecting.

In fact, the light reveals that it isn't *Sarah* at all.

Lying dead in the chair, wearing Sarah's raincoat, is *Kevin*.

TWENTY-TWO

I let out a gasp as the flashlight reveals the truth.

Kevin is *here*—I recognize his face from the profile image on the home swap website.

And he's dead.

It's obvious he's dead, and not just from his lifeless eyes. Buried deep in his chest is the garden fork from the folding table. Blood darkens his shirt till it's nearly black, with more blood pooled beneath him.

"That's Kevin," I stammer, unable to tear my eyes away.

His glasses lie on the ground just beside his head. One of the lenses is cracked.

Larry shakes his head. "What is—"

Bang.

The sharp sound jerks both our heads to the right. It's the same sound that we heard before, the one that woke us up.

Now, I see what the source of it was. It's one of the

bulkhead doors, picked up and dropped again by the wind.

My heart is pounding so hard it makes my chest hurt. That noise can only mean one thing.

The padlock has been removed, and the doors are unlocked.

Larry flicks the flashlight toward the cement stairs, revealing mud and rainwater all inside.

I've reached my breaking point. It's officially all too much.

Questions pelt me, joining a downpour of swirling emotions as I reckon with what's in front of us. I can hardly stand up straight, I'm so delirious with confusion and panic.

Sarah's gone, Kevin's here. And dead. None of this makes any sense.

"That's it. We're leaving," Larry says, swiveling the flashlight to lead us back to the staircase.

"But the roads, the flooding," I say.

He shakes his head. "We'll find high ground and sleep in the car if we have to. I don't want to spend another minute in this house."

We practically sprint back to the stairs, taking them two at a time as we shoot upstairs. Sarah is gone, and Kevin is dead. Not just dead—murdered. Violently.

The gardening tool was jammed nearly up to the hilt in his chest, Kevin's mouth hanging open in a forever silent scream as he lay there on the floor.

I can't get the image out of my head as we stumble back up the steps. Reemerging onto the first floor, I feel lightheaded, like I might actually pass out.

My face is hot, and there are pins and needles shooting throughout my whole body. I lean against the hallway table for support as I suck in a breath.

Larry says something to me that I don't hear.

"What?"

My ears are ringing. Kevin's broken glasses. His lifeless eyes.

"Get the suitcases. I'll start the car and try to clear the driveway," Larry shouts.

The rain pummels the windows with brutal force, as if it wants to come inside and join us. The sky visible through the windows has filled with the first grey light of the morning, enough to illuminate the interior of the house hauntingly.

Below us, the bulkhead door slams shut again, the sharp noise jolting me upright.

A thought crosses my mind that snaps me to a new level of fear.

Sarah's still out there. What she did to Kevin, she might very well do to us if we don't leave—tonight.

We can't wait for the storm to pass or the power to come back on so we can call the police.

Larry tosses his flashlight to the side and goes to the front door, wrenching it open as I grab the stairwell railing with my free hand.

My feet feel like bricks as I make my way up the steps, tripping over myself more than once and nearly sending Sprinkle and myself tumbling down.

There's a candle at the top of the staircase, though it's nearly burned out.

Down below, the front door swings wildly in the

heavy wind, creaking back and forth as rainwater pours inside the front entryway.

I whip my head back and forth on the second floor landing, trying to focus above the noise and panic.

Which room are we in again? I'm so scrambled, I can hardly think straight. Left. Main bedroom.

Stumbling down the hallway, I shove open the bedroom door with a clumsy push and step inside. The windows to my right are painted with rain, letting in only a sliver of the morning light. Its pale glow filters over the room in front of me as I dart my gaze left and right.

Suitcases. Suitcases.

There's mine, half-stuck underneath the bed. Larry's is opened like a book by the closet, some of his shirts still hanging.

I drop Sprinkle onto the bedspread and then get on my knees beside my suitcase, picking up random articles of clothes off the floor and throwing them into the bag.

Moving to the dresser, I yank open the top drawer and remove my underwear and socks. They land in a messy pile on top of my other clothes, but I don't care. I'm not trying to win any packing awards—I just want to get out of here.

The rain continues to pound down outside, wind thrashing it against the glass beside me. It almost sounds as if it's about to give way at one point, but it manages to hold.

Is that everything? I hastily scan my side of the room, conscious of every second I'm spending up here.

It'll have to be good enough. I drop back to my knees

and zip my suitcase closed, having to put my weight on top of it to get it to shut over the bulk.

Larry's is next. I move to the closet and rip down his shirts, sending wooden hangers flying left and right.

Every moment that passes, I wonder if Sarah will appear. What did she do to Kevin?

What will she do to us?

My mind races as I grab hold of Larry's pants and stuff them into his suitcase. I try to close the clamshell lid, but the pile inside is too tall. It won't close.

With a grunt of frustration, I throw it back open and shift the clothes around as quickly as I can.

As I do, I come across something tucked beneath one of his shirts.

It's a phone—but not one I recognize.

Despite the urgency of our situation, I let out a breath as I look down at the phone. The rain and wind rages on outside, but inside I feel deathly still as I reach down to pick up the phone.

I tap on the screen. When it lights up, I gasp.

My hand shakes as I stare down at the screensaver.

This is Kevin's phone, that's immediately clear from the background.

But that's not all.

The screensaver is a picture of Kevin and Sarah.

Sarah's wearing a red Pathmore College sweatshirt. And then it clicks.

Her shirt shows the school mascot, just like Larry's favorite t-shirt.

It's a Phoenix.

Or, in other words, a *firebird*.

TWENTY-THREE

I can hardly think straight as the bright screen burns into my irises.

I don't want to believe it, and yet here is the answer. The reason why nothing has made sense this week. Puzzle pieces are fitting together in the worst way.

Larry and Sarah are working together. Not just working together—*are* together.

She's the other woman, the someone else.

My heart skips a beat as the house creaks and moans around me. My entire body is frozen, my eyes still staring down at Kevin's phone in my hand.

Then the cold realization hits me.

They've already killed Kevin to be together.

What's going to happen to *me*?

Almost as if on cue, I hear the front door slam shut downstairs, and Larry's heavy footsteps stomping across the entryway as he shouts for me in the dim morning light.

"Somebody's slashed the tires," he shouts. "It has to be Sarah."

I stand stock-still in the bedroom, afraid to even breathe. He still thinks I don't know the truth.

"Deb?" Larry shouts again.

He comes to the base of the staircase, his voice carrying upstairs.

"You up there?"

My chest is so tight I'm afraid it might rupture if I move so much as an inch.

My husband isn't just a cheater—he's a killer. A twisted, methodical killer.

If he finds me, I will be next. I know this with more certainty than I've ever known anything before.

Footsteps. Is he coming upstairs?

There's nowhere to run. I'm going to die here like Kevin, locked in a dank basement with my mouth open in a silent scream.

THE SOUND OF FOOTFALLS FADES. Larry's walking through the rest of the house.

Looking for me.

In an instant I'm back on my feet, tip-toeing across the bedroom and coming out into the upstairs hallway, my heart caught in my throat.

My husband continues to shout for me, moving through the first floor.

"Deb, where are you?"

I slink down the stairs as quietly as I physically can, hoping the rain and wind swallow up any noise. Faint light filters in through the windows amid the sheets of rain.

I'm trembling so hard I'm afraid I might miss a stair and go tumbling down. Larry's in the kitchen now—I know because I hear the back screen door open and then clap shut as he shouts for me again.

He's going to kill me if he finds me.

Kill me like he killed Kevin. An image of his shattered glasses flashes across my mind. His face, mouth open, eyes vacant. Blood everywhere. I'm next to die in that basement.

"Deb," Larry shouts again, this time with urgency.

He's walking through the kitchen into the living room. If he turns this way, I'll be spotted on the stairs.

Footsteps, three seconds pass. Two. *One.*

He's rounding the corner, just as I manage to slip around the staircase wall, my breath caught in my lungs.

All that separates us are a few feet of drywall as I hear him cross the entryway and come to a stop in front of the basement door.

"Deb, you downstairs?" Larry shouts.

My pulse hammers in my veins, making my hands throb and my brain ache as I desperately try to figure out what to do next. I blink hard, my sweat-soaked palms clenching and unclenching.

Looking down at them, a chill moves over me. I swallow hard as goosebumps rise across my skin.

The basement door creaks open. Larry shouts my name again as I ball my hands into fists and peek around the wall.

He's on the first step, his back to me. If he were to

turn around now, he'd see me, plain as day. One of his hands is still on the doorframe as he shouts downstairs.

"Deb, what's going on? Are you down here?"

My vision is practically doubled, my heart is beating so hard. I have mere moments. Me versus him.

Rain douses the world around me as I surge forward, bounding across the hallway .

Larry hears me coming and starts to back out of the basement stairwell—but not before I push him back through the doorway with all the strength I have.

TWENTY-FOUR

The force of my shove sends Larry careening back onto the basement stairs' upper landing.

He bounces off the side wall, and then he goes crashing down the stairs, hard.

His body is a ragdoll as he rolls over and over, sickening thuds and crunches filling the air until he finally comes to a stop at the bottom.

My breathing is ragged as I stare down at him at the base of the staircase. He doesn't stir.

A tremble moves through my body as I stand there, the impact of my hands against his back still reverberating through me.

Then I blink and snap out of it. I stagger to the front door, yanking it open.

The wind and rain pummel into me as I look out at our car in the driveway. Just like Larry said, all four tires sag, the air completely emptied.

He really did trap me here.

I'm frantic as I shut the door again, my eyes wide. I take a step back and gulp some air.

I feel dizzy, almost delirious. This can't be happening. I just killed my husband before he could kill me.

Whirling back around, my gaze locks on the basement doorway. I have to go down there, to that horrible place I never wanted to see again.

My throat is dry as I stagger down the steps, sucking in oxygen that doesn't seem to want to stay inside me.

Is he dead? I keep my fists balled as I reach the bottom step, my muscles taut and ready in case Larry jumps at me.

He's lying on his back, face pointed up toward the ceiling. Blood trickles from a cut on his forehead, and one of his wrists is twisted at an odd angle.

I hold a trembling hand in front of his nose... and feel air moving. He's still breathing. Mind racing, I stagger backwards.

What do I do?

I want to leave, call the police, scream. Maybe all three at once.

If he wakes up, he's going to kill me. That's what he was going to do when he came back into the house, I know it.

He and Sarah slashed the tires. There's no escape.

I'm supposed to be dead right now.

My head whips about as I realize that Sarah could be anywhere. She's waiting for Larry to finish the job.

But he failed. I didn't die like Kevin did.

Where is she?

I look again at my husband. The man I tried so hard

to win back. The man who betrayed me in every way possible.

He's unconscious right now. If I decide it, he can be dead.

It's what he deserves, after everything he put me through. I look back at the folding table in the corner. The rest of the garden tools lying on it.

All I'd have to do is take one and plunge it into his chest. Like he and Sarah did to Kevin. He wouldn't be able to stop me.

No. I can't do it.

I can't stop looking at his face.

Even now that the truth has been revealed, even now that I know what he's capable of, I still can't bring myself to end his life.

I let out a hiss of shame.

Despite everything that's happened, some stupid part of me still loves him. How embarrassing is that?

There is literal, concrete proof that he's cheated on me and done much worse, and yet I still can't let go.

Tears burn at my eyes as I grit my teeth. I'm not going to kill him, but I can't just leave him here. Not after the things he's done.

If I leave and he gets up before the police can get here, he might get away with everything. He and Sarah could disappear together.

My eyes are drawn to Kevin and the chair in the corner, my pulse quickening.

Racing over to it, I gingerly pull out the chair from behind Kevin with a wince. His body rolls forward, providing no resistance and allowing me to bring the chair back over to Larry.

It takes almost everything I have to get him into the chair, but I manage it.

Larry's eyes remained closed, a line of blood dripping down his face from the forehead cut. I'm not gentle with him.

Just because I won't kill him, that doesn't mean I'm going to let him off easy. He needs to pay for what he's done.

As quickly as I can, I retrieve the cord from across the room and tie Larry up, yanking hard on it to make sure he's as tightly bound as possible.

Once that's done, I watch him for a second, panting. The house creaks overhead, snapping my head up.

Is that just the storm or is someone upstairs?

I still don't know where Sarah is.

If she's here, I'm in big trouble. I'm totally defenseless. My head drifts to the folding table against the wall, my pulse quickening. The rest of the tools. Hurriedly, I scoop them up. I've got the trowel in one sweaty hand, the shears in the other. I stuff the spade into my pocket, just in case.

My heart bangs against my ribs as I bolt back up the stairs, emerging onto the first floor with my garden weapons at the ready.

I've committed more acts of violence in the past twenty-four hours than I ever thought I would in my entire life. My breathing is ragged as my mind reels.

No one's waiting for me on the first floor. I want

desperately to call the police, but we never found my phone, although now I have an idea why. But maybe...

Rounding the staircase, I bound up the steps two at a time then crash back into the bedroom, head whipping back and forth before I grab hold of Larry's suitcase and throw it up onto the bed.

I'm on the verge of absolute panic, practically hyper-ventilating as I search.

Phone, where's a working phone? I'm pulling clothes out at random, throwing them to the sides as I dig for my phone.

Here's one. Larry's.

I tap rapidly on the screen, but nothing happens. Dead. He told the truth about one thing, it seems.

I toss the lifeless device over my shoulder, hearing it thud from somewhere behind me as it hits the hardwood floorboards.

Another phone. Kevin's again—and his still has some charge left.

I tap on the screen, feeling hope surge through me. Maybe I can call 911 before the battery goes. It's pass-code-protected, but you're supposed to be able to call 911 from any phone, right?

My hands are trembling so hard I'm having trouble swiping on his screen, trying to figure out how to pull up an emergency call button—

And then the phone slips from my grip, my stomach dropping with it as it lands face-down on the solid wood flooring with a sharp *smack*.

My vision blurs a little as I scramble to pick it up, my

gut twisting as I turn the phone over to reveal nothing but pink and white lines on a cracked screen.

It's broken. Unusable. A strangled cry slips from my lips, and then I can't get another breath—it's like all the oxygen in the room has disappeared.

Blinking hard, I turn back to the suitcase as my face burns hot, mirroring the screaming inside my skull that seems to grow with each second I can't find my phone.

Please. It has to be in here. It's my last hope. Please.

Panic and frustration blend together like a toxic potion in my mind, hot tears stinging my eyes as I reach the bottom of his suitcase.

My phone is not here. He probably threw it in the ocean or something.

I collapse against the side of the bed, the sobs I can no longer suppress coming out of me. They get louder and louder, threatening to take over entirely.

My own husband intended to kill me.

Cheating, betrayal, bloodshed—the horror hits me in waves, rocking me to my core as I fight for oxygen against the bedframe.

I want to curl into a ball and give up. Just wither away, fade to black.

Here I was thinking my biggest problem was that my husband didn't love me anymore.

It's way, way worse than that. Everything I thought I knew was a lie.

It's not just the realization that my husband wanted to kill me. It's what that means.

Who am I, if not a wife? No children, no one else to love me.

I truly mean nothing to no one. I am no one.

Just as that thought threatens to take me under completely, another thought flashes through my mind.

More like an image, actually. A collage of little faces, all the children I've taught over the years.

The Billy Ross's, whose lives I've impacted in ways I hadn't even known about. Countless smiling faces. Good people whose lives I helped to shape.

I manage to take in a breath. I'm more than just Larry's wife—I'm a teacher, a mentor. I'm someone.

I am *someone*.

Someone who wants to live. Who deserves to.

Blinking back the tears, I straighten a little, running my hands across my cheeks and mouth.

Think Deb, think.

I need help, but I have no phone.

Rain pummels the windows behind me with force, though there's no more thunder behind the deluge.

Suddenly my head comes up.

Neighbors. They'll have phones, cars. They can help me.

I struggle back to my feet, using the bedframe for support. After picking up the shears, I stumble out of the bedroom, still feeling a little out of my mind.

It's like everything is happening in fast-forward mode, each step quick and darting and disconcerting.

I make my way down the stairs, staring hard at the front door. At any second, I expect Sarah to pop out from behind a wall, another gardening tool in hand.

The house remains quiet around me as I reach the first floor and stumble up to the front door.

Pulling it open, I throw a hand in front of my eyes to shield them from the wind and rain as I lurch outside.

The front yard is practically underwater from all the rain, large puddles covering swaths of grass completely. I can't even see the path to the driveway anymore. I step off the deck and splash down, my feet soaked to the bone instantly with cold water.

It doesn't matter. I just need to find help.

My gaze is drawn immediately to the right, where a glowing window in the distance sticks out from the dim grey of the morning.

Someone has power. Power means charged phones.

I stumble off toward the light, my footsteps heavy and plodding as I race across the yard, sending rainwater splashing as I go. My soaking wet shoes weigh ten pounds each, my thighs burning in protest.

I don't slow down. Now that I'm out in the open, exposed, I can't shake the feeling that Sarah is coming.

She's right behind me, and now she knows Larry didn't finish the job.

My body buzzes with adrenaline that fuels me forward, allowing me to get across the yard to the rock wall that separates the properties.

My leg swings up to climb over it, my wet pant leg snagging on a rough stone and tearing with a loud rip.

Exposed skin tingles as the cold rain splashes down. I get over the wall and land on the other side in another puddle, sinking a few inches deep in the mud.

It wants to pull me down, but I fight through, losing a shoe in the process.

I'm running with only one shoe now, screaming at the

top of my lungs as I approach the neighbor's house. It's built into a hill that slopes down toward the beach. An enormous back deck juts out in front of me, with the glowing window serving as a beacon for my approach.

My body screams at me for rest, but I can't allow it. Sarah's right behind me, breathing down my neck. Underneath every shadowy tree, around every corner.

Just get to the house.

I come up against the side of it, panting hard as I slam on the window with a fist.

"Help me," I scream, bringing my hand down over and over against the glass.

A quick look inside shows an empty living room. It is the crack of dawn, after all. I run down the length of the house to the back deck and climb the stairs up to it, nearly losing my step on the slippery boards.

Righting myself, I run to the back doors and pound on them.

"Help me, help," I scream again, the words burning through my throat.

Where are they? Why does no one answer?

And then I remember—vacation, that's what Billy Ross said.

The power's only on here because they must have an automatic generator. I step back, shivering in the downpour as beads of water roll off my nose.

I rack my brain. *Cheryl.* She and her husband are still in town, though no doubt fast asleep.

Not for long.

Crossing the deck, I leap down the two stairs and land on the soggy grass, taking off toward the cottage again. I can just make out Cheryl's house in the distance, as dark as mine is.

It's all I can do to pray she still has a phone with some battery.

I'm so exhausted, my body utterly drained. I've had less than three hours of sleep in the past two days, but I keep running. I know if I stop now, I won't be able to get going again.

Mental images of the children I've taught push me forward.

If I stop now, I won't ever be able to see them again. I've got to try. I've got to get help.

Over the rock wall I go, and then back into our yard. I splash across it, my legs numb from the frigid water as I heave each foot forward.

The effort it takes is immense, but I'm almost there. I move past our car, which looks like it's sitting in a pond with the amount of water that's gathered around it.

There's only the row of hedges between houses on this side, and I crash through it at top speed.

Branches tear at my shirt and skin, tearing flesh and fabric alike as I tumble to the ground. Mud, water, blood, all cover me in a macabre mixture. I push against the wet grass and get back to my feet, eyes never leaving the yellow house in front of me.

The windows are still covered up for the storm, so I scramble around to the front of the house.

The front door sits quietly flanked by the darkened windows as I reach it, my fist slamming down into the brightly painted wood.

Mud streaks the paint as I hammer the door, screaming at the top of my lungs.

"Cheryl, open the door," I shout.

She and her husband need to wake up—right now. Rain pelts my back, coming down in punishing sheets that sting my muscles with every hit.

I need her to open the door.

Sarah could be anywhere. She could be watching me right now.

I cast a glance around the yard, eyes darting to the corners. If the neighbors don't wake up and answer the door soon, I won't be here much longer.

My fist comes down once more, a sharp pain flashing through my hand at the impact. I'm so exhausted, I can barely stand up straight. My body sags against the door.

And then, just when I'm about to give up hope, I see light from inside the house.

TWENTY-FIVE

"Cheryl," I scream.

The sudden emergence of a glow from inside fills my body with renewed energy. I pound harder than ever.

Since the side windows are covered, I can only peer inside through the foggy glass panel set into the door. There's a bouncing light that seems to be drawing closer —a flashlight, coming down the stairs.

"Help me, please," I scream.

The panel fills with light as the beam is directed right toward it. They're close enough now that I can just make out footsteps as they approach the door.

"—the woman from next door," Cheryl calls out to her husband.

"Yes, Cheryl, it's me," I scream, sounding hysterical even to my own ears. "Please open the door, right now."

There's the sound of the deadbolt sliding, and then the door comes open. I don't wait to be invited, bustling past her the second I have the chance.

Cheryl lets out a shout of surprise, dropping her flashlight which rolls a few feet away.

She's got a robe on, one hand clutching the top half of it together.

"What are you *doing*?" she says shrilly, no doubt alarmed at my sudden intrusion at the crack of dawn.

Where to even begin?

"Kevin's dead. I think Larry and Sarah killed him," I say, the words rushing out of me like water in a flood.

Cheryl's eyes bulge. "Wait, what? Who's Sarah?"

Then, "Larry... your husband?"

I nod quickly, running my hand over my face to sweep off some of the water. I'm sure I look and sound like an insane person right now, but Cheryl can also tell from my body language that something serious has definitely happened.

"Are you hurt? Where's—" she starts but I cut her off.

"Do you have a working phone? Cell phone? House phone?" I ask, my words crashing into each other. "Mine's gone, and we need to call the police right now."

Cheryl starts to nod and then I watch as her eyes widen. She takes off deeper into the house, rummaging around in the kitchen. When she reemerges, she's got something in her hand.

"Is this your phone? I found it on my side of the hedge earlier, just sitting there in the dirt," Cheryl says, offering it to me.

My heart leaps–that's my phone.

"I thought maybe one of the gardeners had left it or something," Cheryl finishes.

No wonder I couldn't find it in the house. My throat

tightens as I finally understand what must've happened. Larry took it, and then threw it over the hedge when I wasn't looking. My chest stills as I realize it was probably left there for Sarah to find, only Cheryl came across it first.

"Thank you–thank you–thank you–" I say, stumbling over my words as I accept my phone with shaking hands.

Please have some battery left. Please.

I've got to get a call off to Billy. I don't remember his number off-hand, but it's saved in my phone. If only I can—

The screen lights up, and a gasp of relief escapes my lips. Panting, I gulp down another breath and try to slow my heartrate.

My phone has seven percent battery left. Nearly dead, but it should be enough to get a call off to Billy Ross. It has to be. Holding up my phone, I swipe it unlocked with a shaking finger.

Squinting, I can just make out the little names in my phone's contacts.

Cheryl's asking me something.

"Huh?" I say, my ears still ringing.

"I said are you okay, are you hurt? Are they still in the house?" Cheryl asks, her eyes wide as she rushes back to the front door to shut and lock it.

That cuts off the rain that was pouring inside, leaving a slick puddle in the entryway.

I shake my head as I try to tap out the letters of BILLY to find his number. I have so many contacts–why do I know so many people?

"I don't know. I mean, Larry's in the basement. I—I don't know where Sarah is."

My hands are shaking so hard, I mess up his name and have to start over. Cheryl disappears into the house again for a first aid kit after noticing I'm bleeding, though it's only the cuts from the shrubs.

Taking a deep breath, I shut my eyes and then open them, doing my best to still my trembling fingers. I've got to do this right.

I take it slow, typing each letter of Billy's name in with purpose as the thoughts continue to race through my mind, pummeling me like the rain.

B.

All of this insanity, organized by my own husband.

I.

Now he's tied up in the basement.

L.

At least, I hope that's where he still is.

L.

My stomach twists suddenly as I realize a possible reason why I haven't seen Sarah.

What if she's down there now, freeing him so they can both come after us?

I finally get his name typed in correctly and press dial. The phone begins to ring as I hold it up to my ear, chewing my lip. I can only hope that's not the case.

If the police arrive and Larry's already gone, I don't know what I'll do.

My eyes flick up to the mantle over the fireplace as I wait for Billy to pick up. There's a vase filled with sea glass among the family photos that decorate the space.

My heart twinges. Memories, shared moments.

All of mine will be forever stained.

The phone continues to ring in my ear as my brow furrows.

I take a step closer to the mantle, phone nearly forgotten as I go for a closer look at the pictures.

My heart beats faster. The lighting is very dim inside the room, but even still...

I blink hard, my throat suddenly going dry. They're lovely family photos, but there's one problem.

The woman in the family pictures is *not* Cheryl.

Then there's a thump—sharp pain—and everything goes dark.

TWENTY-SIX

There is only throbbing pain.

It seems to come in waves, unrelenting. The world around me is black and empty, infinitely large.

Only the steady pulse of pain lets me know there's something beside myself in this universe.

"*Deb.*"

The word floats through the darkness like a lost balloon, moving further and further away until I can't see it anymore. It's faded, lost.

The word comes again, slipping in through some silent door with more urgency. It takes me a moment, but I realize that I know that word.

It has meaning. It's *me*.

In an instant, I'm back, eyes snapping open as I shoot upright.

Cheryl, the photos, everything—all of it is plainly clear in my mind as the strange darkness quickly fades from memory, only to be replaced with real darkness.

It's almost pitch black in here, save for a single wavering candle flame to my left.

My eyes whip about the dark room. Where am I?

I lift my arm—only it doesn't move. A look down reveals why.

Tight cord binds my chest and abdomen, making every breath a challenge.

"Deb, are you awake?"

Larry. That's Larry's voice, right behind me.

We're back to back. Now that he's spoken, I can feel the heat of his body pressed right up against mine.

My arms and chest are bound to the chair with cord in the same fashion as we bound Sarah, and I tied up Larry. I blink hard, tensing and trying again to move my arms, but they don't budge.

"I thought you were dead," Larry says breathlessly behind me.

I try to twist my neck and get a look at him, but I can't. My muscles burn as I turn as far as physically possible, which makes my head throb even harder.

My neck feels wet and sticky. Whatever Cheryl hit me with knocked me out instantly.

The pulsing pain across my skull increases to full volume now, making it hard to focus on anything else as I sag downward, breathing hard.

"What..." I start.

"Oh, good. You're still with us."

The voice from the darkness is sharp, different from the other one.

I blink to try and clear more of the confusion from my

head. That was Cheryl's voice. Behind me, Larry stiffens. I can feel the cords shifting.

There's a soft click, and then Cheryl's face is illuminated from underneath as she shines the flashlight upwards.

It gives her features a terrifyingly haunted look. A human face disconnected from her body as she drifts closer, a look of disgust painted across her features in light and shadow.

"You almost ruined everything, you know," Cheryl says as she comes to a stop a few feet in front of me.

"Let us go," Larry shouts from behind me.

My head pounds so hard I'm having trouble even understanding her. This still doesn't make any sense.

The pain is almost too much. My head sags down a bit, feeling like it weighs a hundred pounds as the world swims.

Cheryl squats and tilts her head up so she can look into my face.

"Don't you get it? You were supposed to call from this house, not next door. No one is supposed to be there," Cheryl says.

She stands back up, her knees popping as she shakes her head. "You were supposed to call the police from Kevin's phone, but I had yours hidden as a back-up. Didn't you hear your phone ringing after you dropped Kevin's phone? I was calling so you'd find it," she continues.

I shake my head, trying to work out what she's saying.

She lets out a breath. "I had to retrieve it and then

hurry back next door to open up with all your pounding and screaming to hand it to you myself."

"I don't understand," I say.

Cheryl scoffs. "Oh Deb... come on, it must be obvious by now. I'm Kevin's *wife*."

TWENTY-SEVEN

The motion hurts, but I lift my head as the shock rockets through me and momentarily replaces the agony in my skull.

Cheryl nods and begins pacing back and forth.

"He was cheating on me with that floozy, and I'm just supposed to pretend it's fine?"

"It was like they were mocking me," Cheryl continues, her voice shifting up an octave, "seeing each other behind my back. Going on trips, laughing. Inside jokes."

She flips the flashlight forward and shines it toward the back of the basement. It illuminates Kevin's lifeless form, still in the same position from when I moved him.

"Who's laughing now, sweetheart?" she says.

A chill runs through me as it all begins to click together. Sarah wasn't the one orchestrating any of this. It was Cheryl.

That's when I notice her shoes—or rather, her boots.

It's the same pair that was under the bed, the boots Sprinkle chewed on. My heart thuds.

Sprinkle.

"Where is he?" I ask. "Where's Sprinkle?"

Cheryl snorts. "Who? The cat? I threw that mangy animal back outside, where it belongs. Serves it right... I've always hated cats. Dogs, too. They're dirty, and they ruin ridiculously expensive boots like *these* with their disgusting little mouths."

She jabs a finger down toward her feet, her lip curling back in disgust.

"*Not* a chew-toy. I actually thought I lost them when I was... getting everything ready. I was losing my mind about it until that cat found them," Cheryl says with a huff.

"They're the only boots I've ever found that help my plantar fasciitis—and that filthy thing was *chewing* on them," she finishes, her cheeks gaining color rapidly.

She runs a hand through her hair and takes a breath. "But that's dealt with. It's all dealt with."

I'm having trouble following her quick, ranting sentences with the pounding in my head. I blink back spots.

After another look down at her dead husband, Cheryl starts moving back toward us.

"It took you two long enough to go downstairs," she says, directing the flashlight at us.

The harsh glow singes my eyeballs and sends a spear of pain through my brain. I wince and twist my head away, but Cheryl keeps talking.

"I figured you wouldn't be able to resist," she says. "After all, it was the only rule. I thought the curiosity about what was down here would've overtaken you much sooner."

"Little did I know I rented this place to two of the most bland, average, rule-following people I've ever seen. I was beginning to lose hope altogether," she continues.

I glance over at her. Why *did* she want us to come down here?

Such a big fuss about the basement, only for there to be nothing but a table and some gardening tools, which...

My mouth falls open.

Cheryl smirks. "There you go. You get it now, don't you? I just needed you to touch one of them, get your DNA on it. Good ole' Larry here couldn't resist."

My injured head pounds as it works through it all. If that's really all she was waiting for, then that means...

"I had to wait until you put DNA on the murder weapon before I could deal with my husband," Cheryl finishes.

My heart thuds wildly in my chest. Wait a minute. What's she's saying... so Kevin *was* here all along.

My thoughts move instantly to the irregular thumping we kept hearing during the night. My stomach twists as my vision blurs.

"The noises..." I say, feeling weak.

Cheryl smirks again. "Kevin always was a fighter, I'll give him that. I was attracted to that when I first met him, actually."

Her laugh echoes through my mind.

"Little *less* charming when he's gagged and bound and stuffed into the subfloor under the kitchen pantry. He didn't make keeping him alive easy, that's for sure."

My entire body tingles.

"But... why?" I ask.

Cheryl throws up a hand. "Are you serious? I needed to deal with getting rid of my husband without recourse. Larry's fingerprints are all over the murder weapon, and Kevin was murdered during your stay. When the police show up, I'll be at my mother's house, as I have been since the separation," Cheryl says.

"There will be no plausible killer other than him," she finishes, "and especially once the motive becomes clear. Larry loved Sarah, who was seeing Kevin. He killed Kevin so he could be with her."

"That's a complete lie," Larry shouts, twisting hard against his binds.

His movement pulls the cords even tighter on my side, making me gasp at the pain when the rope cuts into my chest.

Cheryl smiles.

"Is it though? None of you will be alive to tell the police otherwise," she said. "Deb, you were able to free yourself and kill Larry in self-defense, but not before tragically sustaining a wound that killed you."

"All that'll be left will be some texts and emails between Larry and Sarah, leading the police to draw only one reasonable conclusion." Cheryl holds up a bundle of phones.

I see mine, Larry's, and Kevin's. She's going to manipulate everything so it fits her narrative. A chill runs through me as I stare at the phones.

"The messages from Kevin, the *firebird* email. All of that was *you*," I say.

"I thought 'firebird' was a nice touch. Editing the picture of Kevin and Sarah to make it look like she was wearing the Pathmore Phoenix sweatshirt wasn't easy, but I managed it," Cheryl replies.

All of it was fake. My stomach turns. Larry wasn't cheating on me at all, like he'd been insisting since the very beginning.

He was telling the truth, and I didn't believe him. I let Cheryl manipulate me like a puppet, my insecurities playing right into her hands.

I'm suddenly hyper-aware of Larry sitting behind me, his back and mine separated by mere inches in the dark basement.

He struggles against his binds again, his forceful movements pushing the air from my lungs in a gasp. Finally realizing it, he stops and lets out a heavy exhale.

"You won't get away with this—you're crazy," he shouts.

Cheryl smiles. "I wouldn't say that. In fact, I'm not sure there is a sane response to betrayal by the one you love. Wouldn't you agree, Deb?"

My head drops, my cheeks coloring slightly. Cheryl worked hard to make me think my husband was fooling around on me, and I bought into it.

I can't deny it—I had some dark thoughts about Larry when I *thought* I knew what was going on. Shameful, but true.

"It's a good thing the police didn't pick up your call," Cheryl says. "I still need time to rearrange things. Make everything *look* right, you know?"

She starts to walk away from us, and Larry tries to

bring his arms up, instead of pulling forward. I can hear his strained grunts for almost half a minute before he finally relents.

Cheryl comes to a stop beside her husband's body and flicks the flashlight to look down at him.

In the glow, I can make out the tip of the gardening fork handle jutting out of Kevin's chest. Blood coats the ground around him.

His deranged wife seems to be thinking over something.

"Larry ties him to the chair, tortures him," she says in a contemplative tone. "After he's dead, Larry cuts him loose, and ties up Deb the same way. She's supposed to die next—only she gets free, and stabs him. Yes, that'll work."

Cheryl is plotting out the narrative like some sort of sadistic author, writing her very own thriller in real time. There's this note of detachment in her voice when she speaks about our deaths that sends a line of goosebumps down my spine.

We're not even people to her—just tools like the garden fork, needing to be placed just so.

"All right, then. You two hang tight while I make sure everything looks good upstairs," she says, clapping her hands.

The sharp noise makes me wince, sparkles of pain flashing before my vision.

"Plenty of muddy footsteps to even out and prints to wipe. Need to deal with Sarah, too. Still debating on cause of death there. Writing a story really isn't as easy as you'd think," she says.

She walks back to the candle on the bottom step and picks it up, holding it up at eye level for a moment before blowing it out. With the candle gone, the only source of light in the basement is her flashlight.

Cheryl brings it back over our way. I shy away from the light, not eager to experience another spiking pain through my skull.

"I was planning on saying I'm sorry about all this... but I'm realizing more and more that I'm really not," she says simply before spinning around.

Her footsteps are light as she bounds up the stairs.

At the top, she opens the basement door, allowing a blast of light to filter downstairs.

Then the door is pulled shut, and the room is thrown into total and complete darkness.

TWENTY-EIGHT

I hear Cheryl's footsteps move across the floor overhead as she goes to the front door of the house.

There's a muffled creak, and then a slam as it shuts behind her.

She's going to set up the evidence just perfectly to fit the crime story she's concocted. Move all the pieces into the perfect positions.

Then, she'll come back downstairs and kill us.

The only reason she hasn't done it already, I assume, is that it needs to be fresh, like it just happened after I managed to call for help. I don't know how she's going to make it seem like I'm the one calling for help, but I can think of a couple possibilities.

She could stab Larry, and then me, calling the police while I sputter my last on the ground. All 9-1-1 would hear is my gurgles before I died. She could text people I know from my phone, saying Larry wants to kill me and that I'm hiding in fear.

When no one hears from me in the coming days, they

report it and the police find the two of us dead in the house. Who knows where Cheryl will position us, which narrative she'll decide to go with.

My chin drops to my chest, and my eyes fill with tears.

All of this is my fault. If I had just believed my husband, had some faith in him, we wouldn't be here.

"Can't—get—away—with—this," Larry grunts between jerking movements.

"Larry," I say, my voice quiet as a tear rolls down my cheek.

Everything hurts. Even in the dark, my vision seems to swim.

"There's got to—"

"Larry," I say a little louder, cutting him off.

I feel him come to a rest behind me and hear him take in another breath.

"Yeah?"

"I'm sorry," I say. "I'm sorry I didn't believe you when you were telling me the truth."

Larry wasn't cheating on me at all. It was all Cheryl, dropping little hints and clues that I picked up all too eagerly. My vision pulses.

I nearly killed my husband over something that wasn't even true.

In the darkness, I hear his hair scrape against the top of his shirt.

"No Deb, I'm the one that should be sorry. For everything. You're right—I haven't been putting effort into us. I've been distant, lazy. I started to take you for granted, as ashamed as that makes me to admit," he says.

"Somewhere along the way I just... stopped trying, I guess," he says. "Got comfortable. But as I'm starting to realize, marriage isn't just some machine you assemble once and it runs forever. It's something you tinker with, maintain every day, building it up or breaking it down little by little."

"And I just want to thank you for making me remember that. For reminding me what a marriage should be like," he finishes.

There are tears in my eyes, but no longer from the pain. Despite the immense throbbing in my head and neck, I'm smiling in the darkness.

Beaten, bloody, and tied to a chair, I'm smiling.

"If nothing else, this week has proved to me how much I love you and how badly I still want to be with you... if you'll still have me for whatever time we have left," Larry says.

"Of course I'll have you," I say, fighting back the tears that choke my words.

"Great," Larry says from behind me, his voice barely above a whisper.

There's a creaking, and then I feel his hair brush against mine as he leans his head back. I do the same, careful not to let the spot where Cheryl hit me make contact.

Our heads remain together as a warmth flows through me, reinvigorating me.

"I love you," Larry says.

"I love you too," I respond, shutting my eyes.

And I truly mean it. He is my person, for better, for worse.

Those were the vows we took when we got married, and they mean just as much now as they did way back then.

Larry is my husband, 'till death do us part.

And given that we just found each other again, I'm not sure I'm ready to part just yet.

TWENTY-NINE

Larry fights against the binds again, clearly not ready to give up either.

I try to rack my aching brain. What can we do?

We're tied tightly to chairs in a pitch-black basement in an unfamiliar house in the middle of a thunderstorm.

No way to call for help, no one to come rescue us.

Cheryl will be back before long, and then we'll be out of time completely.

If we don't think of something soon, death is going to part us a whole lot sooner than I'd like.

I shut my eyes again as the sounds of Larry's struggling fill the air. He pushes hard against the cord, but Cheryl knows her knots. They aren't going to budge.

Think Deb, think.

If only we had a way to cut through the cords.

Suddenly my head snaps up, and makes me gasp from the stars of pain that dance behind my eyelids.

Hearing my gasp, Larry stops moving instantly. "What's wrong? Are you okay?"

I nod even though he can't see me. "I think I've got an idea."

"What?"

Licking my lips, I glance off into the darkness.

"The gardening fork," I say.

Everything is silent for a moment as Larry thinks about it. To my mind, it's the only option. Though not meant for cutting, it's obviously a sharp tool, sharp enough to end Kevin's life.

If we can use it to pick and pull at the cord, there's a chance we can free ourselves.

The only issue is of course, that we're bound to chairs on the complete opposite side of the room to Kevin. Not to mention there is zero visibility down here, making any sort of accurate movement impossible.

"Okay," Larry says, breathing out. "Okay, let's give it a shot."

I nod. "How are we going to move?"

LARRY IS quiet for a second as he thinks.

"Spread your legs wide, and press your feet into the ground," he says. "If we both do it at the same time, we might be able to get the chair legs a couple inches off the floor. Then we crab-walk over, okay?"

It could definitely work. Our chairs are bound together, and they're made of solid wood that won't come apart easily.

The rope binding us makes it so what one of us does will affect the other—kind of like marriage.

"Okay," I say breathlessly.

"Lift on three. Three... two...one..." Larry says, the "one" choked with exertion as he tenses up his legs in preparation.

I do the same, my thighs burning almost instantly as I force myself and the heavy chair up with my legs spread as wide as my tendons will allow.

We're actually able to get off the ground—only to land hard a second later as the chair feet come down. The exertion required is immense, and I'm already breathing heavily after one round.

Just that little bit of progress sent my injured head spinning.

But it's try or die. So after another deep breath, I tell Larry I'm ready to go again.

Neither of us is an athlete, especially not at our age. I'm wishing now that I spent more time with the Thigh Master back in the day instead of letting it gather dust.

"Three, two, one," Larry says, heaving hard.

This time, with the force from our legs pushing our backs together, we get up and stay up. One second burns long in my mind, and then the chair legs are touching down again.

I can feel Larry nod in the dark behind me, encouraged. "Okay. We can do this. This time, you try and waddle backwards while I go forwards," he says between gulps of oxygen.

It's an agonizingly slow process, picking up the chairs and moving them mere inches before setting down the legs again. All the while, we've got our ears primed and straining for any sound from above that would signal Cheryl's return.

If she were to come back downstairs now, we'd be finished.

Knowing this, I find energy in my thighs I didn't know I had, and we repeat the process, inching closer and closer.

At least, I hope we're getting closer. As dark as it is down here, we truly can't know for certain if we're going in the right direction.

I'm working from the mental image of Cheryl pointing the flashlight down at Kevin's body as a heading, but with each passing second, the image fades.

My legs are actually trembling now, quivering every time we lower the chairs. Sweat and blood mix on my face and neck.

My sides are sticky as we continue forward, the ropes cutting into my arms.

The tips of my fingers feel cold and dull as I try to grip the base of the seat for support with each lift. The blood circulation to them is limited.

We set down the chairs again, gasping for air. I'm not sure how far we've moved, but it feels like we've been doing this forever. The house creaks overhead, and I flick my eyes up at the ceiling, my pulse skyrocketing.

"Just the wind," Larry whispers.

The house settles and then falls silent again. We have a little more time while Cheryl is busy erasing evidence of my dash across the yards. That wouldn't fit the story she plans to tell.

"Let's go again," I say, refocusing.

Sooner or later, she *will* be back. When that time

comes, she's going to wonder, like we did, what all the thumping is about.

We have to get this done before she gets curious and comes down to investigate the racket we're making.

We lift again, managing two stutter-steps before having to lower back down. I let out a breath, a droplet of sweat dripping off my nose and into my lap.

Survival-mode adrenaline is all that's giving me strength right now, but even that is starting to fail.

It's been too long without sleep, without food. Add that to the throbbing along the base of my skull, and my body is absolutely begging me to stop. To give in.

To surrender.

But I won't. I can't. Not when Larry and I are finally on the same team and working together again.

This marriage won't end in a dark basement—not while I'm still breathing.

"Again," I say through gritted teeth.

We push up, staggering another couple inches across the floor until Larry gasps in surprise, and the legs go down again.

"My foot slipped on something," he says.

"It must've been blood. I think we're close."

I try to look around us, but I can't even see my own knees much less the floor.

There's a scraping sound as if Larry is sticking out his leg and sweeping the ground in a fan motion.

My head comes up as he makes another noise.

"What?" I ask, my throat tight.

"I felt his shoe. We need to turn a little," Larry says.

The discovery gives me the boost of hope my muscles needed to continue.

We shuffle in a half-circle, rotating so that we're in a better position for Larry to feel out the path with his shoe.

"Okay, I think I feel his upper legs. We need to shuffle just a little closer, and then I can grab for the fork with my feet."

We heave the chairs up again, my entire body shaking with force now. But we're so close, we can't give up.

When the chair legs touch back down, my entire body is gasping for oxygen. Larry lets out a grunt as he fumbles with his feet in the dark.

"I think... I think I feel it," he says excitedly.

I hear more dull thumps and scrapes. Larry grunts.

Then—a metallic clatter. The sharp tool is free from Kevin's chest.

"Yes," Larry hisses.

He did it. We've done it.

We made it across the room, and using his two feet, Larry was able to clamp down on the gardening fork handle and pull it out of Kevin's chest.

Now all we need to do is figure out a way to pick it up, and then we can work on freeing ourselves.

My heart soars and immediately comes crashing down again when we hear the front door open and shut overhead.

Cheryl's back.

THIRTY

My entire body goes numb as the footfalls overhead get louder and louder.

Cheryl must be finished outside. If she comes down here now, we won't have enough time to get free of the cords.

My chest aches. All the effort we just expended will be for nothing, all for nothing.

Neither of us dares to move a muscle, our entire beings trained on the ceiling above us as it creaks and groans.

She's drawing closer to the basement door. No, it sounds like she's moving away now, off into the living room. My pent-up breath shoots out in a blast, and I draw another in with shaky relief.

Apparently, there's more work to be done upstairs before she's finally ready to deal with us.

The issue now is that we can't make any more noise. A single thump, and Cheryl will know we're up to something.

I hear Larry straining behind me as he tries to grab hold of the tool with his shoes. There's a sharp intake of breath, and then another metallic clink that spikes my pulse as the fork clatters back to the cement floor.

"Careful," I whisper, my heart hammering in my chest.

We need to be so careful. I listen as hard as I can for any clues from above as to where Cheryl is.

"Sorry," Larry says between gritted teeth as he tries again.

"There's just—blood. Slippery."

He's attempting the near-impossible, trying to pick up the blood-soaked tool between the edges of his shoes and then somehow bring it up to his lap.

And in total darkness.

And we're running out of time.

"I'm gonna try without shoes," Larry whispers.

"Good idea."

I hear his sneakers tap down against the floor as he worms his way out of them.

Every second that ticks by feels like an eternity in my mind. I know that at any moment, we could hear the ceiling creak directly above us and then the basement door opening.

I haven't heard a sound in a while, which almost has me *more* terrified.

Larry lets out a gasp. "I've got it. I picked it up."

My heartbeat quickens, my eyes blinking rapidly as I stare into nothingness. All I can do is listen to Larry as he strains.

The gardening fork clatters off the cement floor again

with a loud metallic tinkle, making my entire body seize up.

Did she hear that?

I can't breathe—all I can do is listen. One second passes. Two. No sounds of commotion.

Larry lets out another exhausted-sounding breath.

"I'm sorry. I don't think my legs are flexible enough to come up to my waist. You know how bad my hip is," Larry says in a sorrowful tone.

I swallow hard, nodding even though he can't see me. It's up to me.

"Okay," I whisper. "Okay, we need to turn. I'll try. Hurry."

We're risking everything by moving the chair legs again. The tool hitting the cement might not have been loud enough to draw Cheryl's attention, but the heavy wooden chair legs dragging across the cement floor certainly would be.

There isn't any other choice though. Any minute now, she'll be back down here, and we'll be out of time.

"As softly as we can," Larry whispers.

"Three, two, one."

We push our backs together once more, and my exhausted leg muscles burn instantly. I fight through the pain, ignoring the flashing lights across my vision as we rotate almost in slow motion.

As hard as I fight however, my body can only hold up for so long.

"Larry," I hiss.

"Okay, lower," he says, understanding immediately.

With my last remaining strength, we manage to lower

the chairs gingerly, so the impact of the legs on the cement is much quieter.

There's only a small thud, but even that makes me wince.

I can only hope it was worth it. Given how dark it is, I've got no idea how much we've turned.

We rotated counter-clockwise, so the gardening fork should be somewhere near my left leg. I'm utterly terrified of kicking it away.

I feel around blindly in the dark with my foot, chest constricting further with each second that passes without me making contact with the tool.

"Can you find it?" Larry whispers behind me.

My face pulses with heated panic.

"No," I say in a strangled whisper.

There is nothing but a sea of black around me. What if while rotating, we shifted too far to the side?

The fork might be an inch past my foot—and forever out of reach.

Despair threatens to take hold of me completely, thrashing my mind with thoughts that scream so loud they nearly overpower me.

I can't allow that. I can't allow that woman to win and callously take mine and my husband's lives just to make hers a little less complicated.

Sucking in another breath I stretch my leg out again, really straining to reach my absolute longest as I do a slow sweep.

There—I felt something.

It's an awkward angle for my leg, but I manage to trap

the tool under my foot, mouth held in a tight line as I draw it across the floor back to me.

It scrapes across the concrete with a low metallic dinging, but that's unavoidable.

And hopefully it's worth it.

Hurriedly I push off my one remaining shoe with the toes of my other one then position both feet so that I've got the fork between them.

Pressing them together, I lift my feet off the floor and begin to slowly bring my heels as close to my groin as I can.

My hands are tied down on my stomach, but I strain hard against the binds as I reach out with my fingers for where I imagine the tool will be.

Everything burns. My legs are utterly exhausted, and this stretch isn't easy.

My heart pulses as the tool nearly slips out from between my feet, but I manage to hold onto it like some desperate, life-or-death claw game.

I'm close, I can feel it.

My tendons burn deep within my legs as I heave upwards, letting out a hiss of air, my wrists tingling as I stretch as far as humanly possible.

And then I feel the tip of the tool. My fingers lock around it, latching on and then pulling it down into my palms with an exhale of utter gratitude.

"Got it," I tell Larry, my entire body flooding with relief.

"Yes," he hisses back, drawing out the *s* sound. "Yes, yes, *yes*."

Flipping the tool around so that the sharp fork edges are facing toward me, I angle it until they come directly into contact with the rope. Then I start moving it back and forth.

A quiet scraping sound fills my ears as the sharp metal begins to separate the fibers of the cord.

My wrists are burning, but I don't slow down. This is it. We're almost free.

There's a snap, and all the pressure against my chest is released.

I take in a huge gulp of oxygen for the first time in what feels like forever, my mind and heart racing with joy and adrenaline.

We did it. I hear Larry pushing to his feet from somewhere behind me as I do the same, keeping one hand on the chair back as I feel around for him.

"Where are you baby?" he whispers.

"Here," I say, "here."

Our hands touch, and a shot of electricity moves through me.

Larry pulls me into a hug, squeezing me tight as the two of us continue to swallow air.

We aren't out of this yet, though.

"Where's the bulkhead doors?" Larry whispers as he takes my sweaty hand.

With my other hand reaching out into the dark in front of us, I inch my way forward until I feel cool concrete on my fingertips.

As I tune in my hearing, I can hear the dull thudding of the rain against the metal doors. They're somewhere to our right.

My pulse quickens. Freedom is so close. We get out those doors, and we might be okay. So close now.

Pulling Larry behind me, I feel along the wall, taking quick steps until there is no more wall. There's only air.

The stairwell opening leading up to the doors.

The rain is louder now, a constant patter overhead. We ease our way up the steps, taking each movement slowly and shakily in the darkness.

Finally, I feel the metal door overhead. This is it.

Larry gets a hand on the doors too, and together we push to freedom.

Except the doors only move an inch or so before all progress halts with a metallic *thunk*.

Cheryl locked the doors again.

My heart crashes down to the bloody basement floor.

The only way out is back up the stairs. Where Cheryl is.

As soon as we start up the staircase, she'll know something is up. I've got no doubt she'll be waiting right outside the door at the top with a big knife in hand, a cruel smile on her face.

But if we don't leave this basement, we're dead anyway. There's no good option.

Larry pants in the darkness beside me. I feel his good hand move along my arm until he finds my fingers.

He squeezes them. "I think I might have an idea."

THIRTY-ONE

My sweat-soaked skin comes up against the hard wood of the chair back.

The ropes are back around my chest. I take a deep breath and then shout at the top of my lungs.

"Cheryl," I scream.

Her name rips up through my vocal cords and out into the unending darkness around me. It leaves my throat a little raw, but I don't stop. I scream her name again and again and again.

I have to pause to catch my breath, leaning my head back until I touch the person leaned up against me in the other chair. Only this time, it isn't Larry. It's Kevin, propped up in Larry's place while Larry hides crouched with the gardening fork in hand.

If Cheryl gets anything more than an initial glance, it'll be obvious Larry isn't the man tied up with me. But all we need is a few seconds.

When she comes down the stairs, he'll stab through

the gaps in the wooden staircase from behind and take her down. It's our only chance.

Drawing more breath into my lungs, I start up the screaming again. We just need to get her down here.

I scream long and loud, really putting everything into each exclamation to try and draw her in.

I don't hear pounding footsteps on the staircase overhead, though. She has to be able to hear all this screaming, right?

So where is she?

A shrill metallic clang answers that question as early morning light floods into the basement from the side. Then there's another light that penetrates deeper, from the flashlight Cheryl uses while she descends the cement steps from the bulkhead doors.

"That eager to die, are we?" she asks in a taunting tone as she steps down from the last step and straightens up.

She pans the flashlight over to Larry, who's crouched in a squat position underneath the main stairs with the fork in hand. He raises up an arm to shield his eyes from the blinding light.

Cheryl knew what we were planning.

My head drops, my stomach clenching.

"I've got infrared cameras down here, you know. The whole house, really. How did you think I found out about Kevin's affair? Or knew which tool Larry had picked up? Or knew you had dropped Kevin's phone like the klutz you are?" Cheryl asks.

She shakes her head. "For a teacher, you really aren't that smart, Deb. Makes me a little worried for the youth."

Larry pushes back to his feet and starts toward Cheryl with a growl, only to freeze in his tracks as she raises up a shotgun. My eyes bulge as the light glints off its black barrel.

Cheryl raises the gun a little higher to showcase it. "Kevin liked to go bird hunting. And not just in the fields, as it turns out."

All of the built-up adrenaline seems to flush out of me in an instant.

My energy is gone completely. There's nowhere else to run, no tricks left to play.

Cheryl has us bested.

We really are going to die here in this musty old basement with no one to hear us scream or know our story.

All they will know is what Cheryl wants them to know.

Tears well at the corners of my eyes again, blurring my vision as I remain seated.

"Okay. Let's get on with this already. Rain's starting to slow, which means they'll have the roads cleared soon enough, and then the police can show up," she says.

Cheryl gestures toward Larry with the shotgun.

"You've already gotten yourself untied, so that saves me the trouble," she says.

The light bounces as she balances the shotgun to reach underarm for something. I notice she's wearing gloves, so none of her fingerprints will be found. A second later, she holds up a plastic bag–and in it, a kitchen knife.

My chest aches. It's the knife I picked up earlier in

the week when we were searching to find out if anyone else was in the home with us.

My DNA and fingerprints are all over it, and Cheryl knows it. She was watching.

When she uses it to stab Larry, it'll look like *I* stabbed him.

Coupled with all the evidence Cheryl has planted upstairs, there's not a chance the police will think we're innocent.

Not like we'll be here to claim innocence or try to explain. By the time they arrive, we'll both be dead.

"Please," I say, standing up slowly from the chair as the ropes fall away.

"You don't have to do this. You've already had your revenge."

Cheryl shakes her head. "No, I haven't. He needs to lose, and I need to win. And I don't win if I go down for this... so unfortunately for you, that means you have to lose, too."

The plastic bag lands with a clunk at her feet. Between the knife and the shotgun, we don't stand a chance. Both of us are exhausted, bruised and bloody, and Larry has a broken wrist.

We're in no condition to fight for our lives.

It's over.

As I look at Cheryl, my eyes are drawn to her boots, the ones she made such a big deal out of earlier.

Not just her boots, the movement behind them.

She seems to notice at the same time I do and looks down.

The movement that caught my eye is Sprinkle, almost

blending with the gray floor and the shadows—and chewing on the boot laces.

His fur is damp. He must have slunk back inside, seeking shelter from the weather when Cheryl opened the bulkhead doors.

Before I can even react, she lets out a hysterical shriek and kicks her leg out, sending the kitten flying with a sharp yowl of surprise.

My heart leaps up into my throat as Cheryl whirls toward Sprinkle, the shotgun raised.

Her face is beet-red with fury—*she's going to shoot that innocent baby*. Everything seems to slow down at once.

"*I said...* these—aren't—a—chew toy—" she screeches, but I can hardly hear it.

I'm lunging forward, mouth open in a scream of my own as I dive for her legs.

Cheryl begins to turn back as she realizes her mistake, that I'm coming for her, but she doesn't make it.

I slam into her knees, bringing both of us down to the floor in a mess of limbs and shouting.

There's so much movement—an arm flies up, more grunting—in my peripheral vision, Larry moving—*Where's the shotgun?*—metal clattering—more screaming—

"Stop." Larry's panting but his command came out loud and clear.

My head whips over to him.

He's got the shotgun, his one good hand on the trigger while he balances it between his knees, holding it shakily as he aims it toward Cheryl on the floor beneath me.

I scramble back up to my feet, backing away from her. A quick check of my body reveals no stab wounds I can see or feel. I think I'm okay.

Cheryl licks her lip and touches blood from the impact of the shotgun butt slamming into her face when I collided with her.

"Deb, come take this," Larry says.

My chest still heaving, I hurry to him and take the shotgun, keeping the barrel trained on Cheryl. It's not as heavy as I expected, maybe seven or eight pounds.

Larry grabs the gardening fork again and pushes himself up to his feet beside me.

After a quick glance back at him to make sure he's okay, I kick away the kitchen knife bag so Cheryl can't grab for it. Then I point the shotgun directly at her.

She snorts. "Oh please. You two are the most mild-mannered people I've ever met in my life. You wouldn't dare."

I shake my head. "You don't know me."

This woman has messed with my entire life. My sleep, my sanity. My relationship with my husband.

And she just kicked my cat.

If there's anyone on the planet I could pull a trigger at, it's this woman.

Cheryl's mouth closes in a straight line as she realizes just how serious I am.

Gone is all the talk about crafting the perfect story. We're the ones writing the narrative now. Not so fun being on the other side.

"What's going on?"

All three of us look over at the bulkhead door steps,

where Billy Ross stands with his service pistol between his hands.

My heart leaps. We're saved! He's here. He got my call.

But then I look where the gun is pointing, and my joy stops abruptly. He's pointing it at *me*.

"Oh please, help me," Cheryl screams suddenly. "They're trying to kill me."

THIRTY-TWO

My heart pounds as Cheryl's desperate cries continue.

I'm shaking my head, but it doesn't look good. I'm standing over her, pointing a shotgun in her face while Larry stands beside me with a weapon of his own.

"Mrs–Mrs. Peterson? Mrs. Walsh? What's... what's going on?" he asks again.

"Help me officer please," Cheryl screams, scrambling back until she's up against the wall.

"She's lying," Larry shouts, pointing at her.

"She's had us tied up down here, look. There's the ropes. She killed her husband."

Billy's eyes flick over to the chairs and ropes and Kevin's body in the corner. His eyes go wide.

"*They* killed Kevin, and now they're trying to kill me. They came here to rob us," Cheryl says in a screaming sob.

She's a blubbering mess now, tears pouring. My chest tightens at how good an acting job she's doing. Is Billy buying it?

His gun is still raised, moving between the three of us.

"Billy, listen to me," I say. "Don't trust a word she's saying. She's—"

"Officer, please, they've already killed Kevin," Cheryl interrupts.

Billy licks his lips and nudges his chin at me. "Drop the weapon, Mrs. Walsh."

I'd totally forgotten I was still holding it. As quickly as I can, I set it down on the ground.

My pulse rushes in my ears. He has to believe us. He has to know we're the ones telling the truth.

The cop takes a careful step forward, glancing over at Kevin again before centering his gaze back on us.

"We didn't do anything," Larry insists. "It was all her."

"No it's all them. They killed Kevin... stabbed him." She points at Larry. "And he's still holding the weapon he used to do it."

All eyes move to Larry, who looks down at the gardening fork in his grasp. It bounces off the floor with a metallic clang as he drops it.

I watch as Billy stares at the fork for a moment before looking back at Kevin's body. When his eyes return to us again, the gun is raised between Larry and me.

My throat closes.

He's buying it.

"Please, you have to believe us," I say, stammering. "All of this was *her*."

But Billy doesn't seem to be paying attention to what

I'm saying. He's taken another step forward, his mouth set in a hard line as his gun remains raised.

"I'm gonna need you to both get on the ground," he says in a commanding tone.

Cheryl takes a gulping breath.

"Yes, yes, thank you officer. They're psychopaths, complete psychos..."

Her eyes shift down to Sprinkle, who's crawled out of the corner and sits near her leg.

"... and they even threatened to kill my kitten if I didn't give them everything they wanted," she finishes.

At that, Billy stops walking. He flicks his eyes down to the kitten, and then—

He points the gun at *Cheryl*.

"Now I *know* you're lying," he says firmly, "Mrs. Walsh loves cats."

I let out a tearful laugh in a rush of relieved air.

Billy remembers the cat posters I had hanging up all over my classroom. They were filled with inspirational quotes and phrases, not to mention some really cute kitties.

Two decades later, and he still remembers.

Larry breathes out too as Cheryl's eyes dart between the three of us, her mistake dawning on her. She went too far in her attempt to divert the blame, and she knows it.

"No, wait," Cheryl says, scooting up a little higher on the wall.

Billy isn't hearing it. He's got the gun trained on her, his entire body tense.

"Don't move," he barks.

Larry and I stumble out of the way as Billy reaches to

his belt for a pair of handcuffs. As they come free, Cheryl begins to protest in earnest.

"You've got it all wrong officer," she screeches, "it's them, not me. *Them*."

Billy gets the cuffs on her and then hauls her back to her feet.

The relief that rushes over me nearly knocks me down. It's like all the stress that's been keeping me upright is finally released, and I'm left to cling to Larry for support.

He throws an arm around my shoulder and gives it a squeeze, holding his broken wrist tight to his chest.

Both of us are covered in blood, dirt, and sweat. Billy pats down Cheryl while she continues her insistence.

"You two okay?" he asks as he glances back at us.

I give him a dull nod. Exhausted, injured, but yes, we're okay.

My husband squeezes my shoulder again, holding me close. More than okay.

"Why aren't they in cuffs? I'm telling you, it's them, not me. They're murderers," Cheryl shouts shrilly, her voice high and pitchy.

"You'll lose your job over this, you realize that, right?" she adds, shifting to threats now as Billy directs her toward the cellar steps.

"Maybe, but I don't think so," Billy says, walking her forward.

"I need you two to come with me as well," he says to us. "The detectives will want to talk to you."

I nod and look around for Sprinkle. There he is, a little ball of damp white fur on the cold cement floor.

Leaning over, I scoop him up and hold him close to my chest. He's shaking.

We shuffle after Billy, our sock feet dragging across the dirty cement floor as we stagger toward the daylight.

It's fully morning by now, and what a morning it is.

The skies, while still a bit cloudy, are backdropped by a shade of orange so bright I wince. It fills in the gaps between the remaining storm clouds, painting them with soothing shades I feared I might never see again.

The world is shiny and damp as we emerge from the house. Everywhere I look, large puddles of water sit.

Branches are scattered everywhere, and there are even a few shingles lying in the dirt to our right. Miraculously however, it's no longer raining. The air is hot and heavy, but free from rainfall.

Larry's arm is around my waist, supporting me as we take the porch stairs one at a time. As we step onto the walkway, I finally allow myself to breathe.

It's over. It's finally over.

"My lawyer is going to have a field day with this," Cheryl says in front of us.

Her boots drag along the wet grass as Billy forces her forward toward the front yard.

"Just walk, please," he says insistently.

We round the side of the cottage and come out into the front yard again. More branches dot the yard, and I can see now that the rock wall separating this house from the neighbor's has sustained some storm damage.

Our car still sits in a large puddle of water, the tires slashed. The windshield has a crack from some object striking it during the windstorm. I expect to see a squad car too, until I remember the roads are flooded.

"The roads are still flooded. I had to leave my vehicle back there and jog over," Billy says with a nudge toward the front porch to direct us.

Larry and I follow Billy as he steps up onto the front porch and sits Cheryl down on the wicker chair.

"Don't move," he says.

"I'm gonna radio for help, and then we're going to get all this straightened out."

Larry and I can do little more than lean against the porch's white wooden support beams. I stroke Sprinkle's back with a trembling finger.

Cheryl shakes her head. "There are the murderers right there, and..."

Her protest trails off, drawing my head up.

I follow her gaze to the yellow house next door, the one she pretended to live in.

The aluminum storm shields have been removed from the windows—Cheryl must have done it during her evidence-cleanup sweep so that the real homeowners would have no idea she'd ever been there.

Now that they're uncovered, it's easy to see what's going on through the downstairs window.

And now I understand why Cheryl was staring with that look on her face.

Because it's *also* easy to see a bloodied Sarah pounding against it with her fists, screaming at us to try and get our attention.

Billy releases the button on his radio as he stares.

"Um..." he starts.

"Why is my girlfriend in the Miller's house?"

THIRTY-THREE

My head snaps toward Billy.

Sarah is his *girlfriend?*

I think back to when we had her tied up in the basement, and she lost her mind when we mentioned calling the police.

We figured it was because she was in some sort of trouble with the law, but this makes just as much sense.

She was terrified of Billy finding out she was cheating on him.

Given the state of things now though, that's the last thing on her mind.

Her pounding against the window only escalates in intensity as she sees us watching her, her cries for help muffled by the walls and distance between us.

Billy takes a step forward, his brow furrowed and his gaze locked on his girlfriend in the neighbor's window. Obviously he's trying to figure out how all this fits together.

Just as I open my mouth to explain, a burst of movement to my left whips my head over.

Cheryl has leapt off the deck and is making a run for it. She knows that Sarah will back up our story, and everything she's said in her defense will fall apart.

She'll spend the rest of her life in prison.

With Billy momentarily distracted, she got the jump on him. Shouts of surprise and warning rise all at once as she races across the lawn, desperately attempting to avoid her fate.

Billy turns and starts to give chase, but then Cheryl's boot jerks to the side, throwing off her cadence and sending her crashing down to the muddy grass. She lands hard in a puddle, face down in the muck.

I can't help but chuckle. All her meticulous planning and crafting, and she's taken down by an untied shoelace, courtesy of Sprinkle's teething.

Billy reaches her as she tries to rise out of the mud and pushes her back down with a knee in the back.

Lifting the tiny kitten up, I give Sprinkle a kiss on his adorable little head.

"You saved the day," I say, smiling.

He lets out a meow, clearly unimpressed. I kiss him again as Larry puts his arm around my waist.

In front of us, Billy heaves Cheryl out of the mud while she continues to fight to free herself. She knows it's over now, but even still, refuses to give in.

The question now is what to do with her until backup arrives. With Billy's squad car still stuck up the road, she can't go in there. He doesn't want her racing off again though, either. After a look at the driveway, Larry offers up a suggestion. Billy ushers Cheryl into the back-seat of our car and then uses another pair of handcuffs to secure her to the base of the driver's seat. Then he shuts the door, cutting off her protests.

She pounds against the windows, but there's nowhere else to run. She's finally cornered, and no longer able to write her own story.

That pen has run out of ink.

After that's settled, Billy looks toward the yellow Miller house beside us.

Sarah's still at the window, watching everything go down. Now that the immediate danger has passed, I can see the change in her body language as Billy begins his approach.

In the distance, I can make out the sound of sirens. The cavalry is coming.

Larry and I settle into the chairs on the porch to give Billy some privacy while he goes to talk with Sarah.

There's still no power, but that doesn't mean there's nothing to watch—not with such a gorgeous sunrise unfolding overhead.

It really is beautiful.

"I can't remember the last time we saw a sunrise together," I say.

Larry shakes his head after a moment. "Me neither. I think we need to change that."

I look over to find him smiling at me. I smile back, my chest warming despite everything.

My head still throbs where I got bashed, but now I know that everything is going to be okay. We're going to be okay.

Larry reaches out a hand. I take it in mine. There's dirt and blood, but there's love there, too.

We sit in a moment of beautiful silence before the sky, watching in awe and gratitude at the incredible showcase above. It's moments like these that remind you just how much there is to live for.

The sirens sound as though they are drawing close. Must've figured out a way to get around the flooded road.

Our moment of bliss begins to fade as the sharp noises draw closer. Soon enough, the first police cruiser pulls into the driveway, lights flashing. Behind it is an ambulance.

The lights reflect off the still-shiny grass, scattering crystals of red and yellow and blue lights all across the yard.

Looking to our left, I watch as Billy and Sarah walk across the Miller's front yard and are met by paramedics. Billy passes Sarah off to them and then starts making his way over to us.

"You guys doing okay? We've got an ambulance here for you," he says as he walks up onto the porch. "You should let them check you out."

I nod. "Thanks again. How did you know to come?"

He nods at me. "Your phone call. I saw I'd missed it and immediately started wondering if something was wrong out here, given the storm and all. Seems like my instincts were right."

My heart beams as I think about his worry for us. Billy truly was—and is—a good kid.

"What about Sarah?" Larry asks.

Billy shakes his head. "She made her choices, can't

say I'm happy about them. Where we go from here... I'm not too sure. I'm just glad she's okay, that's all."

I reach out and give Billy's wrist a squeeze.

"Thank you," I say again. "Really, you saved our lives."

He nods to me, a smile on his face. "I've been meaning to say the same to you for years, Mrs. Walsh."

Tears fill my eyes as we hug. When we separate, I'm still smiling.

Billy excuses himself from the porch to meet up with the other officers on the scene. Cheryl has finally quit thrashing in the backseat of our car, apparently resigned to her fate.

Our eyes meet briefly through the windshield, and then I pull Larry into a hug that I want her to see.

She tried to break us apart, to destroy what we've built together. She failed.

As Larry and I embrace, I know that we'll keep building on that foundation.

Suddenly, all the pent-up emotions from the last week pour out of me and just keep coming until both of us are standing there sobbing as we hold each other.

"I love you so much," Larry says into my ear, and I know he means it.

I nod against his shoulder. "I love you too."

He holds me until the paramedics come up to us to escort us to the ambulance. Even during the ride to the hospital, we continue holding hands.

Now that we've found each other again, we aren't ever going to let go.

EPILOGUE

ONE MONTH LATER

I inhale sharply.

"Careful on the slide, Tim," I call across the playground.

Fourth graders are fearless, and it looks like this one intends to attempt going down the slide standing up.

Tim looks up at the mention of his name and then plants his little butt down the right way and slides down.

I shake my head with a smile. What a little rascal he is. A good kid, though. They all are.

"Mrs. Walsh?"

I look down at my legs, where a little girl named Mia tugs at my dress.

"What is it, sweetheart?" I ask.

She holds up a bow clip for her hair in her small hands. "This fell out."

All around us, the joyous laughter and screams of the rest of the class fill in the background. I smile at Mia then lower myself to her level.

"Let's see if we can't fix that," I say, carefully placing the clip back into her hair.

"There we go. Very pretty," I say, to which Mia beams.

She races off to go join the other kids at recess once again. I sit back, watching them with a smile on my face.

I'd almost forgotten how wonderful it all was, seeing such innocent joy. Such *life*. All these little humans exploring the world, soaking up new information and having a blast while doing it.

And I get to be a part of that.

I take in a slow inhale of the crisp fall air through my nose, shutting my eyes for a moment.

I'm exactly where I'm meant to be.

When my eyes open again, they focus on a man standing at the fence at the back of the lot.

It's Larry, sporting his trench coat and carrying a big bundle of flowers. My heart soars. He sees me notice him and raises his arm up to wave. I wave back, climbing to my feet.

Yes, I'm exactly where I'm meant to be—and I wouldn't have it any other way.

THANK you so much for reading *Don't Go Downstairs*. I hope you enjoyed it. If you'd like to read my FREE psychological thriller novella, The Weekend Trip, sign up for my newsletter at jackdanebooks.com. As a member of my mailing list, you'll be the first to know whenever I have a new book release and get behind the scenes information on my stories and my writing life.

If you had a great reading experience with this novel, would you mind taking a minute to post a review on Amazon? A few words is all it takes, and it will truly make a difference in my career as an author.

Reviews are so important in helping other readers find great books that are worth their valuable time and attention.

Thanks so much for reading :)

Jack

ALSO BY JACK DANE

ABOUT THE AUTHOR

Jack Dane writes thrillers and psychological fiction that largely takes place in New York City, where he lives. When not writing, Jack enjoys going to jazz clubs, taking people-watching walks in the Park, and exploring the city by night, where he picks up ideas for his next book.

Get a FREE copy of his thriller novella *The Weekend Trip* by heading to jackdanebooks.com

You can connect with Jack on Facebook as well!

Printed in Dunstable, United Kingdom